"What are you doing in this house?"

"That's a good question." Rachel stalled for time. Nicholas looked mean enough to chase after her on *two* broken legs. Not that his leg was broken. He'd torn a few ligaments. "Don't you think you ought to sit down?"

"I asked who you are." Nicholas was irritated.

"I haven't decided. Nurse doesn't work. I hate the sight of blood. Cook is so limiting in scope."

"Who the hell are you?" he shouted.

"What would you call me?" she challenged. "Nanny? The closest I could come was baby-sitter, but—" she deliberately swept her eyes over his battered, six-foot frame "—you're not the type women call 'baby.'"

His eyebrows snapped together. "Are you telling me my mother hired you to take care of me?"

Rachel gave him a beaming smile. "Exactly."

Jeanne Allan loves travel, bird- and people-watching, reading, old movies, creative messes, red rooms, her two grown children, sometimes their pets, laughter and anything interesting. Having lived and traveled throughout the U.S. and Europe as a military wife, she and her husband of twenty-seven years now seek the perfect Colorado settings for her books. Jeanne, who was honored as Colorado Romance Writer for 1989, has always loved writing and telling stories, and she hopes her romances leave readers smiling.

Books by Jeanne Allan

HARLEQUIN ROMANCE

Rachel and the
Tough Guy
Jeanne Allan

Harlequin Books

TORONTO • NEW YORK • LONDON
AMSTERDAM • PARIS • SYDNEY • HAMBURG
STOCKHOLM • ATHENS • TOKYO • MILAN
MADRID • WARSAW • BUDAPEST • AUCKLAND

ISBN 0-373-03498-9

RACHEL AND THE TOUGH GUY

First North American Publication 1998.

Copyright © 1998 by Jeanne Allan.

CHAPTER ONE

WARM, noontime breezes carried the sounds of slamming car doors down to the three-story house on Grand Lake. Rachel froze. No. Not yet. He wasn't supposed to arrive until almost noon. She looked at her watch. Fifteen minutes before the hour. She wasn't ready. He'd come too soon. She hadn't worked out a solid plan. Hired yesterday evening, the quick drive up early this morning. She kept thinking there would be more time...

Two voices traveled on the late June breezes. Dyan's voice and a deep male voice with a sharp edge. Had the voice belonged to anyone else, Rachel would have assumed pain caused the sharpness. When it came to Nicholas Bonelli and his current battered condition, his mother and Dyan had been brutally frank in describing son and brother as a bossy, autocratic, surly, ill-tempered martinet.

Nicholas Bonelli. After fifteen years of failing to keep her vow, she'd come up with one last desperate plan. A plan which centered on Nicholas Bonelli helping her.

Rachel stepped back from the window in case he stopped complaining long enough to look up. Although looking up appeared to be beyond his current capabilities. Navigating the rocky path to the front door with his right arm totally immobilized, his right leg in a cast, and a crutch under his left arm probably took every ounce of concentration he could muster. Said concentration not interfering one iota with a stream of curses and complaints. For a second she sympathized with the man hobbling toward the front door, then she remembered who he was.

5

And why she was here.

Through the lace curtain Rachel watched Dyan heave some bags onto the small front porch before retracing her steps up to the road. Passing her stove-up brother, Dyan stuck out her tongue at his back.

"Leave those bags for Charlie," he said irritably. "Even if you did manage to leave your husband and kids in the dust, they ought to be arriving soon." Heavy sarcasm further whetted his voice. "You'd think a cop's daughter would demonstrate at least a token acknowledgment of the fact that we have a speed limit here in Colorado."

Dyan barreled back down the path, luggage hanging from her. Dropping her awkward burdens on the porch, she said, "Give me the key," and jumped up the single step.

The porch roof hid the two from Rachel's watching eyes. She heard the rasp of the key in the lock, then muted voices from the level below. A prudent person would remove the window screen, crawl out onto the porch roof, shimmy down the nearby evergreen tree and run back to Colorado Springs as fast as her legs could carry her. Rachel wiped her sweaty palms on her trousers and waited.

The front screen door slammed. A golden-mantled ground squirrel cautiously making his way around a small boulder froze, his striped body barely quivering. He flashed into a nearby hole as Dyan bounded down the porch step and up the path. Without turning her head she made a thumbs-up gesture over her shoulder in the direction of the window where Rachel stood. Dust settled on the path in her wake. A large yellow butterfly drifted down to a small patch of violet larkspur blossoms. Up on the road a car engine, Dyan's, came to life and roared away. Rachel winced at the screeching brakes and angry honking which marked Dyan's departure. The road sounds faded in the distance. A hummingbird flew shrilly past the bedroom window.

The man below bellowed in outrage.

Rachel took a deep breath and headed downstairs.

Nicholas Bonelli stood in the middle of the huge, open living room. Irritation, frustration and disbelief fought it out on his dark, olive-skinned face. At the sound of Rachel's footsteps, he started, the sudden movement destroying his fragile balance and causing his weight to land on his right foot. The foot encased in a cast halfway up his leg. Sweat beaded on his brow as he teetered on his good leg, fighting to remain standing. A string of curses blued the air.

Rachel stopped halfway down the staircase, locking her hand on the banister to keep from rushing to his rescue. His squared chin and sharp, angled face told her this man always won his battles. Almost always. It took a superhero to best iron and steel. And neon-pink fleece seat covers, came the involuntary thought. She swallowed an inappropriate bubble of laughter.

"You have a nasty sense of humor, lady, laughing at someone else's pain." The rage filling dark brown eyes almost hid the humiliation. "Do you pull the wings off flies, too? Who the hell are you? And what are you doing in this house?"

"That's a good question. Who I am, I mean." Rachel sat on the stairs before her wobbly knees betrayed her. One didn't rush an angry bull. Handicapped as he was, she ought to be able to outrun him, but he looked mean enough to chase after her on *two* broken legs. Not that his leg was broken. He'd torn a few ligaments. Judging by the pain etched on his face, she doubted he'd appreciate the distinction. Reminding herself, he needed her, she locked her shaking hands around yellow-clad knees. "After your mother hired me, I tried to come up with what I should be called." She frowned at the white knuckles gripping the crutch. "Don't you think you ought to sit down?"

"I asked who you are."

"I haven't decided. Nurse doesn't work. I hate the sight of blood. Cook is so limiting in scope. Chief bottlewasher? There's a dishwasher." Forgetting the circumstances for the moment, she leaned forward to add in an awed voice, "When your mother said her 'place at the lake,' I pictured something rustic, maybe outdoor plumbing." Rachel's wide gesture encompassed ten-foot high ceilings, peeled log walls, stained-glass transoms, faded Navajo rugs, oil paintings, the huge rugged stone fireplace, and enough furniture to outfit a lodge. "I can't believe all this."

"Who the hell are you?" he shouted.

His voice, if not the words, put Rachel forcibly in mind of a two-year-old kicking and screaming in frustration as he tested his limits. The shell of the clever, unrelenting bloodhound of big business surrounded a confused little boy who was too proud to admit to his severe pain. Rachel knew all about handling little boys. She raised her eyebrows. "Since when do we yell indoors?" she asked in her best schoolmarm voice.

"Since we want answers to questions," he snarled.

"I always encourage questions. Questions are the sign of a open, active, inquiring mind."

"Thank you," he said dangerously. "I like to think I have an open, active, inquiring mind."

The image of a frightened little boy vanished. A very angry full-size male confronted her. One struggling to control his emotions. If his jaw tightened much more, Rachel feared it would lock forever on him. She knew if she backed down now, she'd lost. "What would you call me?" she challenged. "Nanny? The closest I could come was baby-sitter, but—" she deliberately swept her eyes over his battered, six-foot frame ''—you're not the type women call 'Baby.'''

His eyebrows snapped together. "Are you telling me, in your annoyingly obtuse way, my mother hired you to take care of me?"

Rachel gave him the beaming smile she reserved for students who'd finally mastered the alphabet. "Exactly."

"Forget it. Pack up and get out." Presenting his back to her, he laboriously made his way to the telephone.

She could leave. She could say she tried. She had no intention of going anywhere. "Your mother said to tell you not to bother phoning her. She's monitoring her answering machine and won't pick up if she hears your voice." A ominous silence greeted her words. Rachel resisted an urge to flee.

He slowly replaced the receiver. "Dyan picked a fight with me to have an excuse to storm out. She really is on her way back to Colorado Springs."

"You've got it." She was sure she could outrace him to the front door.

"And Charlie never planned to drive up with his kids."

"Give the man an A-plus. But then, you are supposed to be some kind of hotshot detective, aren't you?" He was the Bonelli half of Addison and Bonelli, the hottest investigative agency around, the one multinational corporations called when they suspected industrial espionage, or insider trading or embezzlement, or any other esoteric white-collar crime, and wanted the matter handled expeditiously, with sensitivity and discretion. And persistence. Nicholas Bonelli was known for never giving up.

He turned slowly and awkwardly around. "If I were some kind of hotshot detective, I'd have figured out who the hell you are, but I don't seem to be able to manage that.'' Weariness replaced the hostility in his voice.

He was going to accept her. She'd overcome the first hurdle. ''Your mother mentioned you'd suffered a concussion.'' She would be generous in victory.

''A slight concussion.'' He shuffled over to a worn wicker chaise longue and carefully lowered his body to the faded, sagging cushion. Laying the crutch on the floor, with the aid of his uninjured arm he swung his injured leg onto the chaise. He leaned back against a mound of pillows and closed his eyes. ''In case you didn't understand me, you're fired.'' Pain seemed to hollow even deeper the flesh beneath high, pronounced cheekbones.

Feeling a momentary stab of compassion, Rachel forced herself to harden her heart. In pain, barely able to move unaided, unable to do the simplest things for himself, he obviously had no intention of giving up without a fight. Everyone had warned her he was a temperamental patient at best. That's why she was being paid an extremely generous wage to dance in attendance on him while he convalesced. No one needed to know she'd have done it for free.

Standing up, she ran lightly down the stairs. ''Dyan said you wouldn't be lunching on the way up. I bought some cold cuts—ham, turkey, roast beef. What kind of sandwich do you want?''

''I said you're fired.''

''You can't fire me. You didn't hire me. I picked up some fresh rye bread on the way up this morning. How about ham and Swiss cheese on rye? Iced tea or lemonade?'' Dyan had packed for him, and she hadn't packed food.

''Who are you?'' he asked wearily. ''The new housekeeper?''

"How about warden? You're in prison and I'm the warden."

Eyelids shot up and startled brown eyes stared at her before narrowing to dark, suspicious slits. "Do I know you?"

"No."

"I didn't think so." He closed his eyes.

Rachel waited a minute. "You never said if ham and cheese on rye is okay. I made the iced tea fresh this morning."

"I'm not hungry. Take your food and get out."

In the kitchen Rachel clung to the edge of the countertop until her knees stopped knocking together. She'd survived round one, but she hadn't won. Not yet. The task ahead loomed higher than the Rocky Mountains, but she could do it. He couldn't escape from her. His mother had made sure of that. She had him where she wanted him. All she had to do was keep him from gaining the upper hand. He was a battered wreck of a man. How hard could it be?

She made two sandwiches. Leaving one on the kitchen countertop, she curled up in a chair in the living room and took a large bite of her sandwich, noisily crunching the crisp lettuce. She crushed a potato chip between her teeth.

Nicholas Bonelli pretended to be asleep. She'd bet his mind was racing to find a way out of his current situation. His mother had tried to close every loophole. Taking advantage of his closed eyes, Rachel studied the dark face beneath short, wavy, blue-black hair. Black eyebrows lent a menacing air, but some women would kill for the ridiculously long ebony eyelashes. Perilously close to his right eye, a red, angry scar clashed with his olive-toned skin. The barest hint of blue coloring his chin suggested a perpetual five o'clock shadow. He looked tough and rugged.

If one discounted the hollow cheeks and high cheek-bones. Rachel's mother would take one look at him and insist on plying him with nourishing foods. Rachel considered his sprawling body. Regardless of what her mother might think, he was neither malnourished nor skinny. He'd separated his shoulder, broken his arm and ripped up his ankle, but even battered, his body spoke of conditioning and wiry strength. Not to mention possessing wide shoulders, narrow hips, and a lean waist.

Rachel chewed her lunch thoughtfully, adjectives springing to mind. Sinister, elemental, primitive. Yet vulnerable and in need of nurturing. Hollywood would cast him as a hardened criminal whose salvation lay in the love of a good woman. She took another bite. According to Dyan, plenty of women agreed with central casting, lining up to be the one to win his heart. Dyan had wished them luck in finding it. Funny how sisters never saw brothers as the object of some woman's passion. Rachel couldn't imagine a woman going gaga over her brother Tony, as much as she loved him. Of course Tony didn't have bad boy sex appeal oozing from every pore of his body.

"You hungry for that sandwich or me?"

Rachel gave a little jump at the dry voice. "Much good a man in your condition would do me."

"Shows what you know." He pulled himself to an upright sitting position and reached for his crutch.

"Can I help you?"

"No. I'm going to raid the refrigerator. Don't worry. I won't touch your food. I'll eat what was here."

"Saltine crackers, peanut butter, instant oatmeal. Eat your gourmet heart out."

"Thank you." He heaved his body upward. "I will."

She would have shoved him backward onto the chaise if she didn't fear worsening his injuries. Instead she stood and blocked his way. "No wonder your mother kicked you out."

"She didn't kick me out." He slowly detoured around her. "I decided I'd be better off staying with Dyan and Charlie."

"Where you ran Dyan into the ground waiting on you hand and foot, not to mention treating Andy and JoJo like unpaid servants."

"I did not—"

"When your mother said you were a pain in the...well, the world's most difficult patient, Dyan assured me your mother didn't exaggerate. The two of them used words like obstinate, impossible, grouchy, certifiable, and those are the ones I can repeat. Dyan muttered repeatedly about justifiable homicide and claimed Charlie locked up his guns to prevent anyone from using them on you."

"I've had enough of you, lady, so—"

"Rachel."

"What?"

"My name is Rachel. Not lady. Rachel Stuart." Carrying her sandwich, she followed him as he made his awkward way into the kitchen. "And you're Nicholas Bonelli, so now we've been formally introduced. Do you want tea or lemonade with your ham and cheese?"

He looked from the sandwich on the countertop to her. "I'm having peanut butter and crackers, after which I'm heading back to the Springs."

"It's a long walk."

Balancing on one leg, his crutch propped against the cabinet, he took the jar of peanut butter from the cupboard. "Someone will come get me."

"Who?" She took another bite of sandwich and slowly chewed. When he didn't answer, she said, "I'm to tell you from your mother and sister that they have begged, bribed, threatened, intimidated and/or otherwise made it very clear to every member of your family, to your every employee and to every person of your acquaintance who has a driver's licence that he or she is absolutely not, under any circumstances, under pain of something awful, to drive up here after you. That includes Charles Addison. You, Mr. Bonelli, have been banished from Colorado Springs for the crime of selfish, extremely offensive and entirely unacceptable behavior as a convalescent. You're to stay here until you're back on both feet and self-sufficient.'' She managed to beam at him in spite of the black look on his face. ''Word perfect. Your mother made me memorize it.''

''Very amusing. Consider me properly chastised.'' He opened the jar, a difficult chore with his right arm strapped to his side. Sniffing the peanut butter, he made a face, and set it aside. ''If you'll excuse me,'' he said with excess civility, ''I'm going to call Charlie.''

''Given a choice between you and your sister, who happens to be Charles Addison's wife, whose side do you think he'll take?''

''Charlie is my business partner.''

''Which is probably why he agreed to Dyan's edict. I heard your employees almost rose in armed rebellion the day you insisted on crawling into the office.'' Still eating, she followed him out of the kitchen, bringing with her the other sandwich.

''I'll hire a car and driver.''

''Good idea. And when you get back to your town house, if you put your mind to it, I'm sure you can manage quite competently even if you are right-handed.'' She bounced a glance off his bound right arm and shoulder.

''My mother doesn't control all my friends. They'll help.''

Rachel set both sandwiches on the large table in front of the windowed wall overlooking the lake and dug into her trouser pocket. "Your mother said she didn't contact any of these names. She said any one of them would be thrilled to offer you care and comfort." When he moved toward her, she edged away, reading from the list. "Yvonne, Tiffany, Sydney, Summer, Allison, Jamie, Jessica, Debbie and Bunnie." She looked up. "I was sure that last couldn't be right, that no grown woman would actually go by the name of Bunnie, but your mother assured me she does. Is she twitchy with a cute little pink nose?"

"Bunnie happens to be a former NCAA swimming champion." Standing by the table holding the sandwiches, he absently picked up the one Rachel had made for him and bit into it.

"Which no doubt qualifies her to play Florence Nightingale."

"At least she doesn't faint at blood. Which you've already admitted lets you out."

"But that's not the most important qualification for the particular job of being your extra arm and leg, is it?"

"You tell me," he mumbled around his sandwich. "You're the one with all the answers."

"The answer's too easy. I'm probably the only single woman in Colorado under the age of forty who has absolutely no desire to become Mrs. Nicholas Bonelli."

He choked on his sandwich.

Rachel returned to the kitchen and poured him a tall glass of iced tea. Back in the living room, she said, "That's not what I want from you at all."

Taking the tea, he gave her a dark look. "Want from me?"

"Not you, precisely." She had no intention of telling him that part. Not yet. "What I want is the job. Your bad temper is my gain. Your mother is paying me an obscene amount of money to keep you out of her hair while you heal. I need the money.''

"Rachel Stuart," he repeated. "I'd remember if I'd met you." His gaze swept over a mass of red, shoulder-length curly hair, salmon pink blouse, yellow slacks and purple sandals. "There's something about your name, but I can't place it. Have you been a client?''

"If I'm desperate enough to take this job, I'd hardly be able to afford the services of Addison and Bonelli, would I?" It hadn't occurred to her he'd recognize her name. Dyan and Mrs. Bonelli hadn't.

He finished off the sandwich, studying her thoughtfully. "Where did my mother find you? Canon City?"

"In prison? As a guard or an inmate?" She laughed with relief. He didn't know who she was. "My kids would definitely say a guard.''

"Kids?''

"I'm a teacher. First grade. That's why I got this job." That and because when Dyan called to say her incapacitated brother was driving her to murder, Rachel had instantly seen an opportunity and leaped for it.

"Because you teach at the same school Dyan teaches at?''

"Because I teach first grade. Your mother thinks any-one who can handle six-year-old boys can handle you.''

Rachel knew the instant the idea hit him.

After her verbal jab lumping him with six-year-olds, Nicholas Bonelli had refused to so much as acknowledge her existence.

Which meant he couldn't object to her carrying his bags into the small, but luxurious, ground-floor bedroom suite near the kitchen. According to Dyan, the room, designed for servants when the summer home was built in the 1920s, had been made over into a handicapped-accessible suite in the late 1970s when Dyan's and

Nicholas's grandmother had been crippled in a fall from a horse she'd attempted to school over a jump. Dyan said everyone had warned her mother's mother the horse had an untrustworthy, nasty disposition, but their grandmother had stubbornly refused to concede any horse could best her.

Rachel placed the last of Nicholas Bonelli's socks in the dresser and closed the drawer with a snap. Nicholas's grandmother had obviously passed her obstinacy down to her grandson. Setting his bag of toiletries in the bathroom, Rachel stared at herself in the large mirror. Mr. Bonelli was about to discover he wasn't the only beneficiary of ancestral stubborn genes.

Straightening the clean towels she'd straightened at least ten times since her early morning arrival at Grand Lake, Rachel considered how best to approach Nicholas Bonelli with her proposition. Done wrong, the whole plan could backfire in her face. She'd never have a better opportunity. She couldn't blow it. If only he were less handsome, well, maybe not handsome by Hollywood standards, but... She groped for the right word. Male. All male. She'd known he had to be smart and personable and clever and a host of other things to be pursued as he was both by women and major corporations. What she hadn't expected was the aggressively masculine virility. Even injured he exuded a sexy animal magnetism which would make any female drool.

Except her. Rachel needed Nicholas Bonelli too badly to be sidetracked by physical attraction. She snorted inelegantly. Nicholas Bonelli ought to be grateful for that.

Gratitude played little part in his attitude as he silently watched her clear the remains from their lunch. He ate without comment the oatmeal cookies she set before him. If he'd asked, she could have told him she'd filled them with all kinds of healthy stuff when she'd baked them last night for him. Leaving nothing but crumbs on the cookie plate, he'd struggled out to the huge screened-in porch and lain down on the daybed. Looking out a few minutes later, Rachel saw his chest rise and fall in the slow rhythm of sleep. Dyan said his pain pills made him drowsy.

Rachel removed her sandals and padded silently up the stairs to her bedroom in search of the book she was reading. A huge wicker chair on the porch beckoned. Quietly curling up on the rose-splashed cushions, she looked out over the lake, her book abandoned in her lap. In the middle of the lake, two sailboats drifted, abandoned by the breezes. A mallard floated tranquilly on the still water, his dark head black in the shadow of a looming evergreen-covered mountain.

Rachel had never been to Grand Lake before, but some pamphlets in the house told of those who had traveled the area in earlier times. Indians, explorers, frontiersmen, miners, hunters, pioneers, farmers and ranchers. Later had come the wealthy to build their fabulous homes along the shores of the largest natural lake in Colorado. The small town of Grand Lake, situated on the north side of the lake near the western entrance to Rocky Mountain National Park was noted for its beauty and summer and winter sports. She wondered if the Bonellis belonged to the high-altitude yacht club. The boathouse attached to the lowest level of the house and the large wooden dock below the deck suggested they did.

An osprey appeared out of the west to fly low over the lake. Suddenly he dove, his feet slashing powerfully through the water, before he rose in smooth, controlled flight. The afternoon sun glistened off the silver fish writhing in the large bird's deadly talons. Repressing a shiver, Rachel felt an odd prickling at the base of her spine. She turned her head to see Nicholas Bonelli watching her.

He said nothing, contemplating her in a way she knew he intended to intimidate her. She raised her chin and refused to look away. Which was how she knew precisely when he came up with his plan. She hadn't taught school for five years, six, if one counted the year she'd practice taught, without learning to read the thoughts going through a devious student's mind. Nicholas Bonelli kept his face expressionless, but he didn't bother to shield his eyes. If he believed Rachel too lacking in perception to follow his thoughts, he was wrong.

Not that following his thoughts required much sagacity. His family had banished him to Grand Lake for a period of convalescence. Banished him with Rachel as his caretaker. As long as Rachel stayed, his family, with a clear conscience, could leave him at Grand Lake. Therefore, getting rid of Rachel had to be his first priority. He couldn't fire her. That left chasing her away.

The tiniest twitch at the corner of his mouth told Rachel his inspired plan gave him as much amusement as satisfaction. She hoped he was as amused when his plan failed miserably. Because it would fail. She never doubted that.

"I've been thinking," he said.

"Good for you."

"You see that as another sign of an inquiring, active mind?" he asked in a mocking voice. Without waiting for an answer, he continued, "My mother correctly assumed I wouldn't ask any of my women friends for help in this particular situation."

"A severely injured ankle would be quite a handicap for a man running as fast as he can to escape the bonds of marriage."

"Do you interrupt the kids in your class every time they open their mouths?"

"Sorry." Patient listening had always been one of her classroom strengths, but while this man's mother might think he'd been acting like a six-year-old, not one of her first-graders had possessed a hard mouth which begged to be softened with a kiss. Rachel blinked. Where had that stupid thought come from?

"As I was saying," he said with exaggerated patience. "Although my female friends would be happy to do a favor or two for me, I don't like to bother them. On the other hand, there's no denying James Donet did a quality job of putting me out of commission. It was probably the first time he succeeded at anything in his entire life." He paused. "On second thought, he was gunning for Charlie, so he even blew his act of revenge."

"Dyan said he deliberately smashed his car into the side of Charlie's car because Charlie uncovered evidence against him."

"The passenger side," he said. "I saw him coming, but we were hemmed in by other traffic, so there wasn't a thing Charlie could do to get out of the way. In my sleep I still see Donet's open mouth yelling words I couldn't hear. And I see those damned pink seat covers in his car." He stared into the sky. "The irresponsible jerk had his kid in the back seat. Fortunately she wasn't hurt. Unfortunately, neither was he."

Rachel could think of nothing to say in the silence following his bitter words.

With visible effort, he sloughed off his anger. "That's old news. What's new is you." He gave her a sultry, hooded look. "You and me, that is."

Rachel wanted to laugh out loud. Did Nicholas Bonelli really think all he had to do was give her a sexually provocative look and she'd run for home? She played innocent. "What do you mean?"

Scorn flickered in the back of eyes browner than the bitterest chocolate before he said smoothly, "I don't know any women with hair like yours. Those red curls are growing on me."

"Really?" Rachel ingenuously wrapped one around her finger.

"I like the idea of a pretty woman at my beck and call. A woman who's being paid—" he emphasized the last word "—to cater to my every whim. I won't have to worry about unwanted entanglements."

"Are you flirting with me?" Rachel looked down at the floor so he wouldn't see the laughter in her eyes. "From what Dyan told me, I wouldn't have thought I was your type." Any woman who breathed was his type. When he didn't immediately respond, she feared she'd given herself away. No one had ever said Nicholas Bonelli was stupid.

"Once while I was hiking up in the Never Summer Range, I found an old green bottle. When the sun shone through the glass it was the same clear green as your eyes."

Startled, Rachel looked at him. A tiny smile played at one corner of his mouth. His scar drew her eye. She wanted to kiss it better. Except he wasn't a scabby, scarred first-grade boy.

"You have a light dusting of freckles across the bridge of your nose. They're cute and kind of sexy." He smiled, disclosing white, even teeth. "Too bad you're not interested in me." His voice deepened. "I've never kissed a redheaded woman. Do men like kissing you, Rachel Stuart?"

Rachel had a sudden, insane urge to have Nicholas Bonelli wrap his tongue around hers the same way he'd wrapped it around her name. Heat crawled up her neck. Dragging her gaze from the gleaming depths of his eyes, she looked across the lake. Dark clouds billowed over the mountains. "I think it's going to rain." On cue, thunder rumbled in the distance. "No wonder it's so hot and steamy, I mean muggy, in here. It must be cooler outdoors." She fled from the screened porch, across the

deck and down the sloping path to the wooden lakeside
dock.

Nicholas Bonelli slowly followed. A stiff breeze
whipped up the lake, and small waves slapped against
the piles under the dock. His crutch thumped across the
dock.

She refused to turn around. She may have temporarily
retreated, but he hadn't won. She wouldn't let him win.

"Did Dyan tell you the famous legend of Grand
Lake?" Without waiting for an answer, he continued,
"Some Ute Indians were camping along the shore when
they were attacked by another tribe. Thinking to save
their women and children, the Utes put them on rafts
which· they pushed out onto the water. A huge storm
suddenly blew up, sending the rafts far out on the lake.
As the braves watched from shore, the rafts overturned
in the rough waves, drowning all the women and children in over four hundred feet of water."

"How awful."

"The Indians abandoned this area for years. Some
say, on dark nights after a storm, ghostly figures of
women and children rise from the water. Crying pite-
ously for help which never comes."

Goose bumps raced up Rachel's arms and she shivered at an eerie sensation of otherworldly creatures
reaching up from the cold depths to grab at her clothes.
"I don't believe in ghosts," she said firmly.

"Such brave words," he said in a low, mocking voice.
"I hope you'll be as brave when ghostly white figures,
shrouded in dripping seaweed, wail and groan outside
your bedroom window at night."

Rachel couldn't suppress an instinctive shudder at his
ghoulish taunt.

He laughed softly. "When they do, don't bother to
come running to me."

Nicholas Bonelli actually believed he could frighten

her away with a silly ghost tale. Rachel turned indignantly to inform him of his error.

He stood closer behind her than she'd realized.

She took a quick involuntary step backward. And fell into space.

CHAPTER TWO

FLAILING at the air, Rachel plummeted downward. She didn't think to scream until she hit the cold, hard water. Then it was too late. Foul lake water filled her open mouth and nostrils, choking her and dragging her down into the depths of the lake. Kicking frantically, thrashing about with her arms, she forced her way to the water's surface to gasp for help.

Nicholas Bonelli stood on the dock bent double over his crutch.

Her body sank like a stone. She was drowning. Drowning in front of a man who laughed uproariously.

While another Stuart died.

Except Rachel wasn't ready to die. She battled the lake, her arms and legs windmilling in all directions. Her frenzied movements propelled her upward and she popped above the water, but the lake refused to relinquish its captive. The water claimed her, as it had claimed women and children before her.

She'd risen above the surface long enough to get a blurred glimpse of the fiend on the dock waving at her. And yelling at her. A farewell address, no doubt. Water filled her ears, deafening her.

The lake wrapped around her in a deathly embrace. Rachel waited for her life to pass before her, but her thoughts stuck on one horrible truth. She'd failed her father.

No. She couldn't, wouldn't, let that happen. Nicholas Bonelli had to undo the damage his father had done.

Rachel clawed her way above the surface, only to

freeze in panic as she realized Nicholas was trying to shove her under with his outstretched crutch.

"No!" she screamed.

"Damn it, reach for it! Grab it, you stupid idiot. Grab my crutch, damn it!"

The loud, angry words finally penetrated her water-logged brain. Latching onto the crutch, she hung on with the last of her ebbing strength as Nicholas towed her through the water.

The dock loomed insurmountably high above her. To come so close to safety only to drown in the dark shadows of the dock pillars struck Rachel as the cruelest of ironies.

"Damn it, let go of the crutch and climb up the ladder."

Rachel blinked bleary eyes at the dark metal steps rising from the water. She couldn't possibly drag her exhausted body up them. A hand grabbed the waistband of her trousers and hauled her out of the water. She landed on a firm male body. A firm male body which gave her a tremendous shove. The wooden dock smacked her backside as she came to rest beside Nicholas Bonelli.

Limp as an overcooked noodle, she lay passively on the dock, half listening to the furious man at her side raging through a litany of swearwords. When he began to repeat himself, Rachel said, "You need to enlarge your vocabulary."

Stark silence greeted her observation. Then he said in a coldly furious voice, "Do not use that patronizing tone when speaking to me."

She'd almost drowned. This man held no terrors for her. Without opening her eyes, she said, "Temper, temper."

A hand closed over her wrist. "If I had any hope you'd drown, I'd shove you back into the lake."

Rachel's eyelids snapped up. Nicholas Bonelli leaned ominously over her. Opening her mouth to tell him to bug off, she saw the water splotches on his shoulder brace. "Oh, no, I landed on your shoulder. No wonder you swore. It must hurt abominably. What can I do?"

"You can tell me what the hell you were playing at," he snarled. "If you were supposed to be a drowning Ute maiden, you overacted." Slapping away her helping hands, he struggled to his feet.

"I wasn't playing. I can't swim."

"All you had to do was stand up and walk to shore. The water's not much deeper than three or four feet where you fell in."

"Oh."

"Oh," he mimicked her feeble response. "I'd like to know what my mother was thinking to hire a lamebrain like you. I've never seen a person panic the way you did. It's scary knowing parents actually entrust their children to you. Some help you'd be in an emergency."

"I'm usually very good in an emergency."

"Yeah, right. You admitted you can't stand the sight of blood, and you have hysterics when you get a little wet."

"I thought I was drowning." As his mouth opened she hastily added, "I didn't know how deep the water was."

Giving her a disgusted look, he hobbled up the path to the house. "I'm not staying here with an incompetent ditz. I'll hire a car and driver to take me back to the Springs. You can stick around here or go home. That's between you and my mother."

She'd proven herself incompetent. No one would fault him for leaving. His shoulder could have separated again when she'd landed on him. Wet and miserable, Rachel wrung water from her dripping clothes. He couldn't leave. Not after all her planning. She'd had the upper hand over Nicholas Bonelli and, because of a stupid phobia, she'd blown it.

She had to convince him to stay. "That was a joke about me hating the sight of blood," she lied, then hesitated. "I admit I'm a little afraid of water."

"No kidding." He kept going.

She attempted to explain. "When I was two, my folks went sailing off the coast of California, and they took me along. My dad tried to get me to wear a life vest, but I threw such a tantrum, he let me have my way, told my mom he'd watch me. One second I was there, the next I'd fallen overboard. Mom said they dove and dove before Dad found me. She said it seemed forever, but I couldn't have been under too long because I lived. I don't remember anything about it, but I don't like water."

Her muttered words halted his plodding progression across the deck. He pivoted laboriously around to stare at her. "I don't suppose you mentioned your little neurosis to Mom or Dyan."

"I didn't think it mattered."

"When you were coming to a lakeside home on Grand Lake? Maybe you thought someone would drain the water for your convenience."

The sarcastic statement brought her chin up. "I don't like to swim. Being around water doesn't bother me. It's not as if I expected either one of us to go into the lake. If you hadn't been harassing me, I wouldn't have fallen off the dock."

He lifted an eyebrow. "I don't recall harassing you."

"You know very well you were trying to scare me away with your stupid ghost story."

"You're scared of ghosts, so you jumped in the lake?"

"I didn't jump. You were crowding me and I fell."

"I suppose now you're claiming I pushed you."

Turning, he maneuvered his body through the open French doors. "I don't know what your game is, Teach, but it's over, so get out."

It couldn't be over. He couldn't leave. She needed his help. "Please." She choked, following him into the house. Clearing her throat, she tried again. "Please. Give me another chance. I need this job."

He turned his head. "Why?"

"Teachers don't make that much money. We count on summer income. I'm paying off a student loan from college."

"What have you been doing since school let out?"

"Odd jobs. Interior house painting and wallpapering. Helped an elderly lady move. Did some cat- and house-sitting." She made a face. "Few people want to hire someone who'll be available only for the summer. When Dyan called, I leaped at this opportunity." Hiring someone to take care of him had been Rachel's idea.

"Why?"

"I told you. Money."

His lips twisted in a cynical smile. "Which means Mom bribed you with the big bucks."

"Yes." He didn't need to know she'd have come for nothing.

"If you stay," he said slowly, "Mom will work it so I end up paying your salary. Make it easier on both of us. Tell me how much she's paying you, and I'll pay you that much to drive me back to Colorado Springs. You can go back to your house-painting and cat-sitting."

"No, you can't. I can't."

"You'd make more money, and making money seems to be an overriding concern of yours. Considering your water phobia, spending a few weeks at the lake can't hold much appeal for you."

"It wouldn't be fair to your mother. It would be like cheating her."

"Cheating." He eyed her thoughtfully. "Are you sure we've never met, Ms. Stuart? Your name sounds familiar."

"Positive." Breezes came through the open doors, plastering Rachel's clammy clothes against her skin. She shivered.

"Go take a hot shower," he said impatiently. He clumped down the hall toward his room.

Ignoring the goose bumps marching over her skin, Rachel hovered indecisively. Nothing had been settled.

"Now!" The sharp command whipped down the hall.

Her sandals squished as she ran up the stairs. She hated taking any order from Nicholas Bonelli, but a shower would give her time to come up with some compelling reasons why he should stay at the lake. With Rachel Stuart dancing attendance on him.

She was in the middle of shampooing her hair when it occurred to her now would be the perfect time for him to run out on her. She blinked soap from her eye. If he did, she'd track him down and break his other arm.

Loud swearwords emanated from Nicholas Bonelli's bedroom. Followed by a loud crash.

Rachel leaped the last few steps and dashed down the hall. Racing through the open doorway, she didn't immediately register the scene before her. When she did, she skidded to a halt.

Six feet of lean, well-built, tanned male stood across the room. Nicholas Bonelli wore two casts, a bandage, a shoulder brace, and a pair of boxer shorts. Her feet riveted to the threshold, Rachel couldn't decide where it was safe to look. Not at bare legs sprinkled with dark hairs. Not at a masculine nipple peeking from dark curly hair. She dragged her gaze downward, resisting any urge to dwell on a taut, washboard stomach, and settled thankfully on boxer shorts covered with childish drawings in vivid colors. "Your underwear is darling," she managed. "JoJo and Andy must have decorated them for you. I recognize the way JoJo draws trees. She painted a picture for my refrigerator."

"Did you come busting into my bedroom to discuss my niece's artistic talents, Ms. Stuart? Or were you looking for a cheap thrill?"

Rachel felt her face turn as red as her hair. She'd been gawking at him as if she'd never seen a half-dressed male before. "I heard a crash. How was I supposed to know you were in here stripping?"

"If you will recall," he said with exaggerated patience, "your theatrics in the lake ended up with you flapping about on top of me like a beached whale. I had to change my clothes. I assumed I was free to do so in the privacy of my bedroom."

Another wave of heated color washed over her face. She'd lain on him for less than a second, but she needed no reminder of how his body had felt beneath her. Safe and comforting. And all male. She thrust aside the disturbing memories. He was deliberately trying to embarrass her. "I thought you'd fallen."

"My briefcase fell on the floor."

Rachel frowned down at the heavy black leather case. "I can't imagine how…"

"I bumped it, okay? I lost my balance and bumped it. Now, if you're finished with your inquisition and through playing peeping Tom, perhaps you'll leave me in peace to finish dressing." His voice changed, the sharp edge supplanted by a seductive drawl. "Unless, of course, you want to help me." He chuckled. "Such a delightful blush, Ms. Stuart."

Rachel refused to let him chase her away. "That's why I'm here. To help you."

"Is it?" Balancing on his good leg, he pointed his

crutch at the massive old wardrobe across the room. "Get me a pair of sweatpants."

She silently complied.

"Put them on me," he said softly, daring her.

He still thought he could drive her away. Rachel had been challenged by too many grade-school boys to be defeated by Nicholas Bonelli. Kneeling on the floor, she gently worked one pant leg over his cast. He sat on the edge of the desk and lifted his good leg. She carefully pulled up the charcoal sweats, trying to ignore the warmth of his skin and the hair tickling the palms of her hand. With the waistband of the pants halfway up his thighs, she stopped and sat back on her heels.

Red flowers and yellow butterflies danced in front of her eyes. Dyan was always bragging about her children's creative endeavors. Their uncle's undershorts had to be one of their finer efforts. Rachel admired the choice of colors, the way a rabbit seemed to bound toward her. Her cheeks grew fiery hot as she belatedly realized the rabbit's placement on the underwear. "Okay," she said in a strangled voice, "you can finish."

"You want to remember those big bucks my mother is paying you to grant my every wish and command," he said. "You finish."

If much more blood rushed to her face, the top of her head would blow off like a volcano. Rachel gritted her teeth and tugged his pants up to his waist, trying not to dwell on the bumps and curves of the male anatomy. Stretching the elastic waistband, she released it with a hard snap.

Stomach muscles flinched.

Rachel rose. "What shirt do you want?" She didn't bother to hide the triumph in her voice.

"Pick one," he said impatiently.

Opening a drawer in the wardrobe, Rachel selected a stone-colored sweatshirt with chopped-off sleeves and a zippered front. She eased it over his injured arm and shoulder and carefully zipped it shut.

Nicholas Bonelli watched her with hawk eyes. Except for one involuntary wince, he might have been carved from stone.

"There," Rachel said brightly. "All done." Before she could step back, an arm whipped out to hold her in place.

"We're definitely not all done, Ms. Stuart." He reeled her closer.

Taking unfair advantage. She could hardly kick or slug a disabled man. "You want shoes and socks?"

"No, Ms. Stuart, that's not what I want." His arm tightened. "I don't think you have enough freckles to be a natural redhead." His fingers caressed her side. "But I like your mouth. Wide, generous, not too red, not too pale. Just the right shade of pink, like strawberry ice cream. Do your lips taste as good as they look?"

"I don't know." Her every breath pulled in the musky, masculine scent of his soap, and her mouth trembled under the heat of his heavy-lidded gaze. The edge of the desk bit into her thighs as he pulled her between his spread legs.

"When I don't know something," he said softly, "I have to investigate." Leaning nearer, he barely brushed the tip of his tongue against her closed lips before drawing her bottom lip into his mouth and sucking on it. "I'm driven by curiosity."

The muttered words tickled her lips, and then his mouth closed over hers, bathing her with moist heat. She stood very still, unable to move for fear of hurting him. He shifted slightly, the movement causing his shoulder brace to brush against the sensitive tips of her breasts. Rachel clutched his uninjured arm to hold herself steady, grounding herself. She was a puppet, and he controlled the strings. Passivity was foreign to her nature, however, and soon she matched him, kiss for kiss, eager to explore his mouth. She touched the side of his face, careful not to aggravate his scar. Stubble rasped against her fingers.

Rachel knew a sudden urge to feel the prickle of his whiskers against her lips. His breathing quickened as she skimmed her tongue and then her lips across the dark shadow of beard on a small patch of skin near his mouth. Every part of her body, every muscle, every cell, felt exquisitely alive. Restless longings unfurled deep within her.

"You presented me with quite a puzzle." Nicholas Bonelli nibbled her earlobe. "But while you were showering, I figured this whole deal out."

Rachel snapped back her head. "What deal?" He couldn't have figured it out.

"When I tried to bribe you to drive me back to the Springs, you should have leaped at the deal if you're in it for the money. Unless you're holding out for more money."

Nicholas Bonelli's voice remained as soft, his touch as sensuous, but the hand curved around her chin and the thumb stroking her bottom lip had lost their power to make a fool of Rachel.

Her stomach churned, no longer with desire, but with anger. At him for playing games with her and at herself for being such a naive fool. Nicholas Bonelli had his pick of beautiful, sophisticated women. Only an idiot could believe he'd be attracted to a freckle-faced, red-headed schoolteacher.

Not that she wanted him attracted to her.

Hoping she looked cooler than she felt, Rachel deliberately reached up to the hand resting possessively on her chin and removed it. She almost hoped he'd resist. A swift kick to his injured ankle would go a long way toward evening the score. Instead he smiled, a smile which told her he guessed her thoughts and enjoyed thwarting her.

She stepped back one step. Any more and he'd think she was afraid of him and running away. Her direct gaze took on his mocking eyes. "I'm not holding out for more money. Your mother hired me to do a job. I promised her I'd do it, and I intend to keep that promise. Whether you like it or not."

He didn't believe her for a second. "Dyan's embroiled you in some crazy, Machiavellian scheme, hasn't she?"

"No." Dyan knew nothing of Rachel's plan.

"I've been roped into enough of her lunatic brainstorms to recognize the warning signals. Was pretending to enjoy my kisses part of her plan or were you embellishing? Hoping a few kisses would sway me into letting you stay so you wouldn't disappoint Dyan. Oh, yes," he said, misunderstanding her start of surprise, "I knew you were faking, Ms. Stuart. You ignited too quickly to be credible."

Rachel stamped out her relief before he read it on her face. Later, in the privacy of her room, she'd deal with the awful fact that she'd actually enjoyed kissing Nicholas Bonelli. Now she laughed, he was so far from guessing the truth. "I was afraid you'd notice my kisses were a little forced, but you didn't give me much to work with," she lied. "All those dreadful clichés. For your information, my hair is naturally red, but I don't feel compelled to prove it. As for my lips, the color is available at any local discount store. And there's nothing you can say about freckles I haven't heard before."

"Enjoy your insignificant moment of triumph. You'll be out of here by noon tomorrow."

"I see." She couldn't remember why she'd been laughing. "You intend to call your mother and tell her I panicked. She'll think I'm not qualified to take care of you and she'll fire me.'' Rachel clenched her fists at her side. Her plan rendered useless because she was stupidly afraid of a little water.

"I don't exploit people's weaknesses, Ms. Stuart. Your secret little phobia is safe with me." He toyed with the clown pendant hanging around her neck. "I don't need to go that low to get what I want." Amusement flickered across his face. "In less than twenty-four hours you'll beg my mother to let you quit."

She studied his face for signs of trickery or deceit. He eyed her steadily back. Arrogance rode his high cheekbones. Challenge glittered in his eyes. Oddly enough Rachel believed he wouldn't use the one weapon he could use against her—her deadly fear of water. He didn't need to.

Rescuing her necklace, she moved away. If Nicholas Bonelli wanted a fight on his hands, so be it. To the victor, who would be Rachel Stuart, would go the spoils. "Short of assaulting me or pushing me into the lake to drown, there's nothing you can do to force me to quit."

"Maybe you better stay indoors. And away from me."

Rachel shook her head. "You're not the type to take the easy way."

A smile reeking of masculine superiority and arrogance slowly curved his lips. "If you're basing your conviction on your experiences with first-grade boys, Ms. Stuart, I assure you, I am not six years old."

She matched his smile. "I assure you, Mr. Bonelli, I never thought you were." She started from the room.

His voice stopped her in the doorway. "One other thing, Ms. Stuart. Even if my expertise doesn't meet with your approval, there was nothing underhanded about my kissing you. I kissed you because you have kissable lips. Can you say the same?"

The unexpected statement astonished her. She flushed

pink with pleasure, before realizing he was softening her up so she'd lower her guard. She sent an artlessly blinding smile across the room. "I'm sorry, I can't. Your lips aren't particularly kissable." She didn't stick around to see if he believed the lie.

"I wasn't asking you if my lips are kissable." His shouting followed her from his room. "I was pointing out that at least my kisses were honest, which is more than you can say."

Rachel leaned on the deck railing. "Kissable lips," Nicholas had said. Her lips looked pretty ordinary to her. Her mouth was too wide. Generous, her mother said, but Gail Stuart put a positive spin on everything. She'd even managed to retain her optimism when her husband had died on the heels of his being accused of sabotaging the company he worked for. Rachel wished she had half the strength of her mother. If she had, she would have cleared her father long ago. And not be standing here mooning over some dumb kisses and an idiotic remark made by a self-centered man who thought the entire world had come to an end because he'd suffered a few petty injuries.

A plopping sound and a flash of silver distracted her. The fish disappeared, only the spreading concentric ripples on the water's surface marking where he'd risen to feed. A couple of boats departed the marina, the smell of gas from their engines drifting across the lake. A common merganser glided past the dock, his black and white body cleaving silently through the pollen covering the water. Rachel sipped from her coffee cup and burrowed deeper into her emerald green fleece robe. The mercury on a nearby thermometer hovered around forty, but the early morning peace and quiet compensated for the chill.

Rachel hoped Nicholas Bonelli liked to sleep late. He must have exhausted himself yesterday dreaming up ways to run her ragged. She'd driven into town to check the family box at the post office. When she'd returned, he'd remembered he wanted a local newspaper from town. When she'd come back with the newspaper, he'd dropped it on the table while he railed about the quality and quantity of food in the refrigerator. Fulfilling his dream grocery list had required two more trips into town. Then he'd changed his mind about what he wanted for dinner, and she'd driven into Grand Lake again. She'd cooked the spaghetti he'd requested, when he decided he'd rather have pizza from town.

Rachel came close to refusing to go for pizza, but the look in Nicholas's eyes told her he wanted her to refuse. She wouldn't give him the satisfaction.

Any more than she'd give him the satisfaction of knowing his kisses had come dangerously close to up-setting her plans. Kissing wasn't what she wanted from Nicholas Bonelli. No matter how mind-numbing those kisses were. Mind-numbing because she was an idiot and he was an accomplished Lothario. Only a fool would believe he'd kissed her because he'd been attracted to her lips. He'd kissed her to manipulate her into carrying out his wishes.

"Where's my breakfast?"

Coffee splashed down the front of Rachel's robe. "Don't sneak up on me like that."

"People on crutches can't sneak. The way you jumped, a person would think you had a guilty con-science."

"Why would I have a guilty conscience?" she asked defensively.

"Because you're not paid to stand around like part of the scenery. You're paid to take care of me. I want breakfast, and I hope the coffee doesn't taste as bad as the look on your face says it does." He eased himself into a deck chair.

Rachel's fingers tightened on her mug. It was almost laughable the way he tried to hide his pain. Nicholas obviously considered himself too macho to admit he hurt. She had to fight to keep from wanting to comfort him. He had plenty of women for that. All he wanted from Rachel was her absence. An absence which would force his family and friends to care for him. An event Rachel had no intention of allowing. Nicholas Bonelli wasn't going to chase her away nor was he going to wear her down. "What would you like to eat?" she asked sweetly. "Pancakes with powdered sugar and arsenic?"

He gave her a cool stare. "If the job's too much for you, you can always quit."

"I have no intention of quitting."

He raised a doubting brow. "I want scrambled eggs cooked with a little onion, cheese and kielbasa sausage."

"We don't have any kielbasa sausage. I assume you want me to drive into town to get some?"

"You're getting paid the big bucks."

All the way to town and back, all the time she chopped and mixed and beat and cooked, Rachel occupied herself with inventing novel ways to murder one Nicholas Bonelli. No wonder Dyan's husband Charles claimed he'd been driven to lock up his guns.

She relished her one minor triumph, the look on Nicholas's face when she'd returned from the store and he'd asked for the newspaper and she'd whipped one out of the grocery sack. Thereby derailing the order on the tip of his tongue that she return to town for a newspaper.

She carried out a tray with steaming hot eggs and two perfectly browned pieces of toast. "Orange marmalade and black cherry jelly." She set the tray on the lakeside table.

Nicholas eyed her blandly over the top of the newspaper. "I hope that's not for me. I got hungry while you went to town so I fixed myself a bowl of cereal. I don't want anything now.''

A man could be smothered in scrambled eggs. A person of less patience and less determination might be tempted. Rachel smiled gamely and returned the tray to the kitchen.

He called to her before she could set the tray down. The liar. He hadn't had breakfast. She carted his breakfast back outdoors. He gave it a dismissive look. "You know what I need?"

"Yes."

Laughter briefly gleamed in his eyes. "Teacher, teacher," he chided. "I was under the impression corporal punishment went out with slate tablets." He faked a cough. "My throat is getting dry from hollering for you all the time. I need a bell or a whistle. Like the call button they have in hospitals to summon nurses."

"Certainly, Mr. Bonelli. Did you have a specific kind of bell or whistle in mind? No, don't tell me. I'll drive into town and buy something suitable, and then, if I buy a chrome whistle you can always say you want a silver bell or vice versa."

"The job too much for you, Ms. Stuart? You can quit."

"Why would I quit? I love frustrating, petty little tyrants." Better petty tyrants than the man who'd quickly grasped what she'd meant by her answer to what he needed. She'd almost won a genuine smile of appreciation from him. Not that she wanted smiles. She wanted him to heal. A process she hoped they both survived.

Back in the kitchen she stuck the eggs in the refrigerator. What Nicholas needed was something to take his mind off feeling sorry for himself. And off trying to get rid of her. Maybe now was the time to approach him with her proposal. No, not yet. Let him continue to believe Dyan was hatching some wild scheme, although what kind of scheme he could possibly think Dyan would involve Rachel in, Rachel couldn't imagine.

The insulting answer immediately popped into her head. Of all the conceited, egotistic, self-centered males. Stomping back outside where he sat, half dozing, in the morning sunshine, she said hotly, "I haven't the slightest interest in you as a man."

He opened his eyes. "I'm devastated, of course. What the hell are you talking about?"

"You think Dyan has some cockeyed scheme to pair me up with you and I'm going along with it. For your information, I'm not the least bit interested in a man who has one-dimensional relationships with women. Other men select their clothes to match the occasion, but you chose your women that way. Dyan's told me how you take Jamie to the symphony and play handball with Tiffany and sail with Debbie and go dancing with Yvonne."

"How sad teachers lead such dull, uneventful lives that you have to spend your lunch breaks discussing my social life."

"We don't discuss you."

"You learned about Jamie and Tiffany and Debbie by osmosis?"

"You forgot Yvonne. Not to mention Summer, Jessica, Allie, Sydney and of course, Bunnie."

The startled look on his face turned speculative. "For a woman who claims a total lack of interest in me, you've apparently made it your business to find out a great deal."

Rachel could have smacked her runaway mouth. Why couldn't she think before she blurted out nonsense? Now she had to admit she needed him to clear her father's name. It was too soon. She wasn't ready. The groundwork hadn't been done. She took a deep breath.

The ringing of the front doorbell saved her.

CHAPTER THREE

THE boy standing at the front door had a small bandage strip on one elbow and a smear of what appeared to be grape jelly on his cheek. He gave Rachel a solemn, blue-eyed look and gravely announced, "I need to talk to the cop."

"I'm sorry," she answered with equal gravity, "but there's no policeman here."

The towheaded youngster frowned at her. "I know he doesn't live here, but I saw the car so he's here. It's real important I talk to him." The boy screwed up his face, fighting off tears. "Scotty's gone."

"Scotty? Your brother is gone?"

"Nah." Disgust dried his tears. "Just because it's his birthday today and he's having some dumb ole party, Mom's gotta bake a cake so she can't go look till it's over and that'll be too late cuz he's not good about cars and I'm not allowed to ride my bike on the highway so I need the cop, don't ya see?"

Rachel tried to sort through the information the boy had flung at her. "Today is Scotty's birthday?"

"No," he howled, "it's dumb Eric's birthday. He's six."

She thought she had it now. "Eric is your brother and Scotty is your dog and he's run—uh—disappeared."

"Yeah," the boy said with relief. He waited expectantly, confident that now Rachel understood the problem, she'd solve it.

She hated to disappoint him. "Maybe your mother could call the local police department or dog catcher."

"She don't wanna bother them. I'm getting my own

41

cop.'' He scowled. "He tole me he was a cop in Colorado Springs.''

"Lt. Bonelli,'' she guessed. Nicholas's father.

"Yeah. We fish together." The boy stared at Rachel's purple slacks. "Sorta. He fishes and Scotty and me, you know, kinda hang around." He added earnestly, looking up into Rachel's face. "He likes Scotty, he really does. Says he's smart enough to be a police dog."

"I'm really sorry, but honestly, Lt. Bonelli isn't here. He's back in Colorado Springs. The only ones here are myself and…" The solution blinded her with its utter brilliance. She needed more time. Nicholas needed something to occupy his mind besides his pain and enforced inactivity. The boy needed help. She opened the door wider. "My name is Rachel. What's yours?"

"Ian," he said dispiritedly.

"You're in luck, Ian." She motioned him to come in. "Lt. Bonelli isn't here, but his son, who's a hotshot detective, is here. He'll be glad to help you." Rachel would make sure of it.

"A detective?" Ian asked in a awed voice. "Like on TV?"

"Exactly." She led the way through the house to the deck. "Nicholas, a fishing buddy of your father's is here to see you. Ian, this is Nicholas Bonelli."

Ian turned to Rachel, his eyes huge. "What happened to him?" he asked in a stage whisper. "Did a bunch of bad guys try and kill him?"

"That's the risk you take when you're a hotshot detective." She gave Ian a warning look. "Don't ask him about it," she said out the side of her mouth. "It's top secret. He'll act like he doesn't know what you're talking about. All you need to know is he solved the Case of the Fuchsia Fleece."

Nicholas glared at her. "Would you mind telling me what's going on here?"

Rachel exchanged conspiratorial glances with the boy. "Ian has a problem you'll want to help him with."

"Will I?" Nicholas asked in a voice which clearly conveyed she couldn't be more wrong.

"I'll get some cookies and lemonade," Rachel said. When she returned Nicholas wore a look of total bewilderment as Ian bombarded him with information in his eagerness to explain the dire nature of his problem. "Scotty is Ian's dog," she inserted helpfully, setting glasses of lemonade in front of each male. "According to your dad, Scotty's as smart as a police dog."

"If he's so smart," Nicholas snapped, "how'd he get lost?"

Rachel gripped the plate of cookies so hard, she marveled the plate didn't break in half. "What Nicholas means, Ian," she said levelly, "is there must be some other reason Scotty hasn't returned home." Her next words came out coated with ice. "Isn't that right, Nicholas?"

Nicholas opened his mouth, caught sight of Ian's wobbling bottom lip and visibly swallowed whatever he was going to say. Shooting Rachel a look which promised later retribution, he said, "All right, Ian, let's start over at the beginning." As the boy wiggled impatiently, Nicholas added, "That's how I work." Grabbing a cookie, he pointed it at Ian. "I'm a hotshot detective, and you're my client, so we gotta do this my way."

"Who's she?" Ian asked around a mouthful of cookie.

"My bimbo secretary. All hotshot detectives have bimbo secretaries. I call her Dollface."

"Cool." Ian leaned forward. "Are you guys like on TV? Ya know, she just wears her underwear when you're talking?"

Nicholas choked on his cookie. "How old are you?"

"Eight."

Rachel serenely sipped her lemonade. Nicholas obviously hadn't paid enough attention to his niece's and nephew's conversations. Children's minds flashed here and there, and one never knew the direction their next questions would take. As a bimbo secretary named Dollface she was undoubtedly too dumb to take offense. He would have hired her for her long legs. She glanced down at her chest. Yup, it must have been for her legs. Her hair wasn't even blond.

"Okay, Dollface, you drive while Ian and I scan the woods along the road. Stop every hundred yards or so, and turn off the engine. Ian'll call Scotty. Everybody listen hard to hear if the dog answers. Think you can handle that?"

Nicholas's unexpected sense of humor had caught Rachel unaware. Dyan could be hysterically funny, and Mrs. Bonelli had displayed a whimsical sense of humor during Rachel's job interview, but Rachel had assumed Nicholas seriously lacked a funny bone.

If her discovery of Nicholas's sense of humor hadn't quelled any irritation at being called Dollface, the look of hero worship on Ian's face would have. Once he'd grasped Ian's problem, Nicholas had focused his considerable talents to solving it. Gone was the fretful, demanding patient. In his place was the clever, dedicated, incisive Nicholas Bonelli, whom international corporations called upon for prevention and detection of high-dollar, white-collar crime.

Nicholas had snapped out orders for pencil and paper, sketched the area, mapped out probabilities, phoned Ian's mother and spoken with the sheriff's department. "You know your dog," he'd said to the young boy straining at the bit to begin their search. "Get inside his head. We have to think like Scotty. Where would he go

when he got loose? What would he be looking for? What
are his favorite things?"

Scotty had disappeared from the backyard while Ian
and his brother accompanied their mother to the grocery
store. The dog had dug a hole under his fence. Without
hesitation Nicholas had agreed the dog undoubtedly had
gone looking for Ian.

They'd searched the streets of Grand Lake without
success. Other areas Nicholas ruled out because of rough
terrain. Now they cruised slowly southwest on Highway
34 hunting for any sign of the missing dog. The local
law had assured Nicholas no strays or dead dogs had
been reported. Rachel prayed they wouldn't find a small,
still body beside the road.

"Don't get discouraged because we didn't find him
in town," Nicholas said. "If he got loose when you
think he did, he's been roaming for several hours. Dogs
can cover lots of territory."

"He chases squirrels and cars. That's why Dad hadda
build a fence. He says Scotty is stupid, but he ain't. We
didn't know much stuff when we was eight months old,"
Ian added defensively.

"A puppy who doesn't know a stranger." Nicholas
spoke in a musing voice. "I remember a puppy I had,
that little fellow could put on a starving act two seconds
after he'd been fed. When the neighbors ate outdoors, it
was all we could do to keep Frank home. Dollface, turn
into this picnic area up ahead."

Rachel dutifully followed Nicholas's instructions.

Halfway along the parking loop, Ian shrieked, "Stop!
There he is. I see him."

Rachel hit the brakes and looked around. Nowhere did
she see a small puppy. Ian shot from the car shouting
his dog's name. Frenzied barking erupted from a nearby
picnic table. Rachel thought her eyes might pop out.

"Do you see what I see?" she asked faintly, eyeing in disbelief the huge black dog greeting Ian.

"When Ian described his puppy as 'kinda big,' I assumed what seemed big to Ian wouldn't actually be that large." Nicholas shook his head. "That's not a puppy. That's a horse." He unbuckled his seat belt. "Help me out of the car. Ian seems to be having trouble reclaiming his dog. Although I can't imagine why anyone else would want that monster."

By the time Rachel and Nicholas joined the group at the picnic table, Ian was picking furiously at the sturdy knot in the rope securing the huge, boisterous dog to the wooden table. "Scotty is, too, my dog," Ian shouted over the dog's barking. "He is. Tell him, Nick."

Before Nicholas could open his mouth, Rachel burst out indignantly, "Look at that dog. Of course he belongs to Ian. He's about to wag his tail off." Not to mention deafening them with his sheer joy at seeing Ian.

"Yeah, well," the man said, "he went just as crazy over my wife when she handed him a hot dog. Poor fella was starving to death. How come he's out running around these woods?"

"He dug under the fence to search for his master." Nicholas frowned at the barking dog. "Quiet. Sit."

To everyone's amazement the dog sat and grinned a silent puppy grin, his tongue hanging to the side.

The man crossed his arms over his chest. "If he belongs to the kid, how come he's not wearing a collar?"

"It got too small. Mom said he'd choke."

Rachel had a feeling Scotty had outgrown a whole host of collars.

Leaning on his crutch, Nicholas pulled out his billfold and extracted a business card. "I'm Nicholas Bonelli. Ian hired me to find his dog. I think you'll find any number of witnesses willing to testify the dog comes from a good home. If you still have doubts the dog belongs to Ian, why don't you check with the sheriff? There's a phone box right over there.''

The man thumbed the card, looking from it to Nicholas. ''He hired you to find a dog? Addison-Bonelli Investigations sounds expensive.''

''Ian's dog is priceless,'' Nicholas said.

''He looks like a mutt.''

''He's not a mutt,'' Ian said in a mulish voice. ''The lieutenant says he's smart as a police dog.''

''Ian has connections with a man high up in law enforcement,'' Nicholas said smoothly. ''The lieutenant might like the idea of felony charges, but I—''

''Felony! You hear that, Marge?'' the man appealed to his wife. ''We feed a starving dog, and they're saying we stole him.''

''No one's saying that. Ian and I appreciate your rescuing Scotty, don't we?'' Nicholas frowned at the boy until Ian nodded sullenly. ''It's impossible to repay you for your kindness, but I would like to reimburse you for the cost of the food you fed Scotty.'' He handed the man some money.

''Yeah, well, the dog was hungry and he seemed nice enough. Marge kinda took a liking to him.''

Rachel gave the woman an incredulous look. Surely the man was joking. As if to prove her husband's point, Marge moved over to pet Scotty goodbye. The dog dribbled saliva all down the woman's bare leg. Anyone with a lick of common sense would pay Marge to keep Scotty, not return him. Judging from the look on the man's face, Nicholas had been more than generous.

It wasn't until she'd opened the car door for Nicholas that Rachel realized she was expected to allow the slobbering behemoth in her car.

''You could have tied him to the bumper. I'd have driven slowly. It's obvious he's been in the lake and rolled in things I don't even want to think about.'' She pulled out of the picnic area. "He's drooling down my neck. Do something."

"He likes you, Rachel," Ian said earnestly. "He usually only drools on people who have food."

The dog reared up in the back seat and placed one enormous paw on Rachel's shoulder.

"He's in love. Pull him off her, Ian, and say 'down' in a very firm voice before we run off the road." Nicholas didn't bother to conceal the amusement in his voice.

Back at the house, the puppy detoured carefully around Nicholas on his crutch. Seeing Rachel, he woofed cheerfully and jumped up to plant his huge feet on her shoulders. His tongue swiped her face.

"Yuk. Get down, you big clown." Rachel grabbed the puppy's feet and placed them firmly on the ground. Straightening up, she braced her fists on her hips. "Now you listen to me, dog. I do not want you jumping on me again. You hear me?"

Scotty grinned at her and vigorously shook his entire body.

She was right. He had been in the lake. Rachel wiped her face again and glared at the dog. "Enough. You behave yourself or I'll..." What did one do to over-exuberant puppies?

"Make him stand in the corner?" Nicholas inquired.

"She wouldn't do that. She's funning. You like Scotty, doncha?"

"Like him? He is the most misbegotten, ill-favored, ill-mannered, incorrigible bag of dog bones I've ever met."

Ian grinned. "See? I tole you she likes him."

Nicholas burst out laughing.

For a split second Rachel's heart literally stopped beating. Muttering something inane about boys and dogs and a shower, she dashed into the house. Not until the warm water cascaded over her did she allow herself to analyze what had happened. Nicholas Bonelli as a tin-pot dictator was one thing. Nicholas Bonelli as a human being was something else entirely. When he'd kissed her yesterday, she'd felt the physical attraction, but she hadn't been in danger of actually liking him.

Rachel squirted more soap on her sponge. Who would have thought brown eyes brimming with amusement and a laughing mouth could be so unsettling? Unsettling? Rachel gave an unladylike snort. When he laughed, a certain tall, dark, ruggedly handsome, scarred and bat-tered investigator turned into the sexiest man she'd ever laid eyes upon.

Being physically attracted to Nicholas was not part of her plan. She furiously lathered her hair. Neither was liking him. She wanted Nicholas Bonelli to clear her father's name. She didn't want to succumb to his con-siderable masculine charm.

She refused to succumb. She refused to be another name in his little black book. How would he categorize her? Rachel, alias Dollface, good for looking for lost dogs? No, she knew exactly how he'd label her. Afraid of water. The means by which his family had temporari-ly banished him from his home and office. Soapsuds stung her eyes. And when she finished with him, the blackest entry of all. Rachel Stuart, daughter of Marvin Stuart.

"You didn't mention Marv Stuart was your father."

Rachel put down her sandwich, her appetite gone. "Should I have?" she asked carefully.

"Not necessarily. You obviously don't hold it against my dad. I know," Nicholas said, forestalling her com-ments, "waiting on me is just a job to you because you need the money. Money doesn't explain your friendship with Dyan."

When she'd met Dyan Addison, Rachel had had no idea Dyan's maiden name was Bonelli. "Did Dyan say something to you about my father?" Dyan had never mentioned him to Rachel.

. He shook his head. "While you were in the shower, after Ian's mom picked him and Scotty up, Dad called." Nicholas took a swig of iced tea. "Mother just got around to telling him this morning that she hired you. He was relieved to hear we're getting along so well."

"You told him we were?" she asked in astonishment.

"You think I'm going to admit a redheaded school-teacher has me pinned down? Temporarily," he added with a scowl. He forked a bite of fruit salad and pointed it at her. "I knew I'd heard your name before. Dad was pretty shook up at the time, because of what happened and with internal affairs investigating. He seldom talked about work at home, but he and Mom discussed the case a lot. I couldn't help but pick up a little about it. Dad was heartsick about you kids. I don't remember your brother's name, but I was reading something by the ecol-ogist, Rachel Carson, for school then, so your name stuck with me. The point is, I don't care what your dad did."

"Nothing." Rachel clenched her shaking hands to-gether beneath the table's surface. "He didn't sell secret bids to Parker and Thane's competitors."

Nicholas raised his brow. "He told you that?"

"My mother told me. He was framed."

"If you say so," Nicholas said noncommittally. "Any of those peanut butter cookies left?"

"Don't you want to know who framed him?"

"No. I want to know if there are any cookies left."

"I see." Rachel carefully tore the crusts off her bread. Waiting for the right moment, she'd put off bringing up the subject of her father. Realizing now there was no right moment, she was almost grateful Nicholas had forced her hand. "I guess your father told you all about the case."

"I remembered a little from when it happened. He filled me in on the rest."

"What did he tell you?"

"There's no need to rehash old news. I wouldn't have brought it up, but I want you to know, my trying to get rid of you has nothing to do with your father."

"What did your father tell you?" she repeated tightly.

After a long moment, Nicholas shoved his plate away. "Marv Stuart worked for Parker and Thane, builders of projects nationwide such as shopping centers, high-rise buildings and airports. They're noted for quality work, fair prices and finishing jobs on time."

He went on. "Which made them wonder when they started losing jobs to other firms. They didn't suspect sabotage at first. It wasn't always the same firm who submitted a bid just below Parker and Thane's sealed bids. But, after two years, when the same three firms kept winning the jobs Parker and Thane bid for, Robert Thane, the founder's grandson and company president, grew suspicious. He called in the police, but they found nothing. No one suspected a valued employee like Marv Stuart."

Nicholas continued steadily, "It was the merest co-incidence Thane opened a drawer in Stuart's office to borrow a pencil and found a copy of the firm's latest sealed bid. A bid which had no business being in Stuart's desk."

Rachel's stomach knotted. "You forgot to mention Robert Thane wasn't alone."

He gave her a quick glance. "My father was with him."

"He didn't have a search warrant. He had no right to go through my father's desk."

"Dad admits if the case had gone to trial, that evidence might have been a problem."

"But it didn't go to trial, did it?" Rachel forced herself to meet Nicholas's gaze. "Because your father killed mine. He conveniently hit him with the police car when my dad stepped into the street."

Her last statement hung accusingly in the air.

"Dad was right," Nicholas said flatly. "Your taking this job wasn't a coincidence, and it doesn't have anything to do with money. What do you have in mind? Shoving me off the dock, hoping my casts will pull me under? Or is it going to be a butcher knife during the night?"

Rachel opened and closed her mouth in shock. Finally she managed, "You think I'm planning revenge?"

"You tell me."

"I want to hire you."

It was Nicholas's turn to be stunned. "Hire me for what?"

"To clear my father."

He was shaking his head before the final word left her mouth. "All the evidence was against him. Dad said he proved conclusively your father was the only one who could have put that bid in his drawer."

"No, he wasn't." The knots in her stomach intensified. "Two other men could have." Before Nicholas could ask, she blurted, "Robert Thane and your father."

Nicholas threw his napkin down on the table and pushed back his chair. Rising awkwardly, he grabbed his crutch and braced it under his arm. "I'm going to lie down for a while. This morning wore me out."

An admission he'd never have made if she hadn't rattled him. Guilt and uncertainty about her planned course of action crept in. Nicholas' injuries were hardly imaginary. The minute she'd come down from her shower she'd noticed his brow furrowed with pain and his face gray-tinged with exhaustion.

She'd blown it. Her timing stunk, and instead of gradually working up to her proposition, she'd blurted out serious accusations against his father. Even a man in excellent health would hardly jump with joy when someone insinuated his father had framed an innocent man and then murdered him to cover it up.

Slowly gathering up the remains of lunch, Rachel wondered if Nicholas would call someone to drive him back to Colorado Springs or expect her to take him.

He slept through the dinner hour. He must have taken more pain pills. It irritated her she felt guilty about bothering him now. He was the one who'd brought up her father. To reassure her, a little voice said. Rachel ruthlessly stamped out the voice. Her conscience didn't bother her one bit when it came to Nicholas Bonelli. Even if he was injured and in pain.

He'd been a big pain. Practically shoving her in the lake. Forcing her to allow a big, filthy galoot of a dog in her car. The memory of Nicholas's laughing face caused her throat to painfully swell. She'd never see him laugh like that again.

A rock dug into her side. Rachel pushed it away.

"Ms. Stuart."

The irritated voice calling her name came in concert with renewed prodding. Rachel forced up heavy eyelids. Nicholas stood beside the chaise, balanced on his good leg, poking her with his crutch. "Stop it, go away," she muttered, batting at the crutch. Closing her eyes, she turned her back to him. A sharp poke in the middle of her spine brought her furiously upright. "Quit poking me. What do you want?"

He put the rubber tip of the crutch back on the floor.

"I want breakfast and I want to know why you're sleeping down here instead of in your bed."

"I fell asleep reading," Rachel lied, pointing to the book on the floor. She'd slept downstairs in case he woke during the night and wanted something to eat. She doubted he'd believe or appreciate the gesture.

He glared down at her. "You, Ms. Stuart, are the most worthless nurse or whatever the hell you're supposed to be, it's ever been my misfortune to encounter." His nostrils flared in disgust. "I can't believe you slept all night in your clothes."

She no longer had to appease him. He was going to fire her. And make it stick this time. She yawned in his face. "I don't suppose you made coffee."

"It's your job to make coffee. Comb your hair before you start. You look like hell."

Rachel stretched. "You're no morning glory yourself. You're not getting any breakfast until you shave."

His eyes turned into thin slits. "I see the perky little veneer has worn off, allowing your true personality to shine through. I use the word 'shine' loosely."

"Are you always this grouchy in the morning?"

"If you can't take it, Ms. Stuart, you can always quit."

If he called her Ms. Stuart in that cold, nasty tone of voice one more time, she was going to slug him. Belatedly the meaning of his words struck her. She stared up at him. "I assumed I was fired."

"I fired you the first minute you walked down those stairs, but I haven't noticed it's had any discernible effect whatsoever on your leaving."

"You're not firing me," she said slowly.

"You're not listening. I fired you two days ago."

Rachel impatiently brushed his claim aside. "Why aren't you firing me? After yesterday, I expected..." She shrugged.

"Expected what, Ms. Stuart? That I'd call my sister or my parents or Charlie and tell them you're clearly delusional and a threat to my health?"

"Something like that, yes."

He leaned over his crutch, his gaze pinning her to the chaise. "I don't need help getting rid of you, Ms. Stuart. You think I've been irritating so far? You ain't seen nothing yet." Nicholas's eyes spit fury. Red spots of anger highlighted his cheekbones and picked out his healing scar. Wrath oozed from every pore in his body. "I'll bet by dark you'll be running back to the Springs."

Rachel should have been intimidated. She wanted to giggle. The man wore a restrictive brace on his shoulder, casts on a leg and an arm, and even with a crutch, he could barely hop. The accident and his painful recovery left him as dangerous as a week-old kitten. Swallowing her amusement, she said, "I'll accept that bet, Bonelli. I'll even raise the stakes. You win—I drive you back to Colorado Springs. I win—" she inhaled deeply "—you clear my father's name."

Nicholas's face darkened. "I told you. He's guilty."

"Chicken." She made clucking noises.

"My courage has nothing to do with it."

"Not that I blame you for being afraid," Rachel said. "If I dreaded what an investigation might turn up on my father, I'd refuse to investigate, too."

"I'm not afraid. My father is an honest man."

"Then you have nothing to lose by investigating the matter."

"I'm not interested in wasting my time on pointless, quixotic crusades."

Rachel studied her fingernails. "You must not have much faith in your ability to chase me away," she said in a offhand tone of voice, "since you're afraid to bet."

"I don't have to prove my courage to you, Ms. Stuart." He added softly, "Or my masculinity."

She blinked at that, but said only, "No, all you have to prove to me is my father committed the crime. And prove his death was an accident. Since you won't be able to do either, you'll be proving his innocence. Which I guess you're afraid to do, for fear of the consequences." His eloquent silence told her the juvenile challenge had failed. She shrugged. "You can't blame me for trying. I'll hire someone else."

"Good luck."

"I'm not interested in public justice or pillorying the guilty party. I want the proof of Dad's innocence for my brother. And Mother. She says he's innocent, but sometimes—" Rachel forced her voice to remain level "—I think she has some niggling doubts and those doubts tear her up." She cleared her throat. "Never mind. You're not interested."

"I am interested to know why me. I'd think I'd be the last person you'd ask to investigate."

"I thought you might have a stake in the matter. Seeing as how he's your father and all."

"Why don't you tell me what you're leaving out?" he suggested evenly.

"All right. I'm leaving out money. It's true what I said earlier about needing money to pay off college loans. Dad left us nothing. He would have," she said quickly, "but he didn't know he was going to die so young. Mother married him right after they graduated from college, and she'd never held a job outside the home. She soon found out her degree meant nothing in the job world." Rachel gestured aimlessly. "Oh, she found a job. Enough to feed us, clothe us, keep a roof over our heads." A mirthless smile bent her lips. "We ate a lot of soup and peanut butter."

"I don't see—"

"I don't have the money to pay another investigator. I'd hoped to persuade you to investigate for free."

Nicholas gave her a sudden, sharp look. "Forget about persuading me," he said coolly. "As you pointed out, my social calendar is already full."

"What does your social..." Heat rushed to her face as his meaning hit her. She leaped to her feet. "That's as disgusting as it is arrogant. I'd never use sex as a means of persuasion."

"What then?"

"If you investigate, your findings go no further than me and my family."

A motorboat roared noisily by on the lake. "And if you hire another investigator?"

The icy, controlled voice dispelled any notion Rachel might have harbored of a weakened, defenseless convalescent. Incapacitated or not, Nicholas Bonelli gave off exceedingly dangerous vibes.

"I can't afford another investigator." Her hands curled at her sides. "I'll go to the newspapers."

His knuckles turned white where he gripped the crutch. "I don't appreciate blackmail, Ms. Stuart."

She threw up her head to meet his black gaze. "I have to fight with the weapons I have. Wouldn't you do as much for your father?" His eyes barely flickered, but Rachel knew her question hit home.

"You wouldn't be able to control what a reporter dug up or what he did with the information," he said slowly.

"I know."

"You'd be gambling with the reputations of Dad and Thane. No matter what they'd done or not done, they'd undoubtedly come out of it with some mud clinging."

"I could have gone to the newspapers first instead of coming to you."

"Is that what you would have done if this little job hadn't fallen into your lap?"

"I read an article in the newspaper several years ago about you and Charlie and your company. You both refused to be interviewed, so it was a small article, but there was enough to tell me you two had become the leading experts on white-collar crime. That's when I got the idea of having you investigate what happened. I've been trying to meet you ever since. Twice Dyan had parties and I expected to see you there, but you were away on business.''

"You could have called me on the phone.''

"Your private number is unlisted. I knew I wasn't important enough to make it past your secretary.''

"I suppose you know Dyan well enough to know she'd throw you out on your ear if you mentioned this to her.''

He wouldn't believe her, but Rachel told him anyway. "I chose not to involve her.''

He raised his eyebrows in disbelief. "Naturally.''

"Listen, Bonelli,'' Rachel said heatedly, "I'm twenty-seven years old. For the last fifteen years I've lived with the knowledge that my father was accused of a crime he didn't commit, and that he died because of that crime. That hurts. Regardless of what you think of me, Dyan is my friend, and I don't want her to suffer the same way.''

"You think going to the newspaper won't hurt her?''

Rachel closed her eyes briefly. "Sometimes in life—'' she selected her words carefully "—a person has to make choices. A friend or a father. Friendship or honor. Making difficult choices doesn't mean a person likes them.''

"Suppose I said I'd investigate on one condition.''

His tone of voice put her on guard. "What condition?''

"I'm not a charitable organization, Ms. Stuart. I don't give away my investigative services. On the other hand, you said you're forced to fight with the weapons you have.'' A cold, contemptuous gaze swept her body. "I doubt a woman who favors apple necklaces and teddy bear socks could interest me in bed, but maybe you have hidden talents. You could trade your services for mine.''

CHAPTER FOUR

HIS words might be open to interpretation, but the sneer on his face left no doubt in Rachel's mind as to Nicholas's meaning. "No, thank you. I'm not interested in your help under that condition." If she couldn't control the flush tinting her face and neck, at least she managed to keep from shrieking at him.

"It seems you aren't quite as anxious to clear your father as you claim."

"I'll clear him. With or without your help. And without doing anything which would shame him if he knew about it."

"Such noble sentiments," he mocked, "from a criminal's daughter."

The blood drained from Rachel's head, and she grabbed the back of the nearest chair for support. "So much for not holding my father's crime against me," she said in a low, fierce voice.

A muscle tightened in his jaw. "I apologize. I shouldn't have said that. We both seem to have spoken without thinking. You said, 'my father's crime.' Could it be, down deep, you don't really believe in his innocence?"

"Don't be ridiculous."

"That would explain why you set yourself up for failure. You must have known from the outset I wouldn't agree to help you. And I very much doubt you will find a reporter interested in a fifteen-year-old crime in which charges were never filed."

"Because your father killed mine."

"Your father dashed out from between two parked

cars and ran right in front of Dad. There was no way Dad could stop in time. He was cleared of any wrong-doing.''

''By other policemen.''

Nicholas gave her an exasperated look and limped toward the kitchen.

She'd failed. She'd gone about persuading Nicholas to reopen the case all wrong and she'd failed. She may as well pack now. After she made Nicholas Bonelli his darned breakfast. ''Sit down before you fall down,'' she said irritably. ''I'll make the coffee. I want to be able to drink it.''

Without a word Nicholas lowered himself awkwardly into a worn leather club chair. Dropping his crutch on the floor, he closed his eyes. Beneath long lashes, pain drew his skin tightly over his cheekbones, emphasizing his scar.

In the kitchen Rachel took from the refrigerator the scrambled eggs she'd made the previous morning and stuck them in the microwave to reheat. As much as she disliked Nicholas, she'd been hired to do a job, and until she was replaced, she'd do it.

Nicholas Bonelli had been her best hope. She wasn't so naive she didn't realize he was right about the news-papers. What had happened fifteen years ago was old news. Even then, the only mention of her father in the paper had been his obituary. Parker and Thane had hushed up the incident, and apparently whoever committed the crime had been scared off from doing it again. Fifteen years later, Parker and Thane flourished.

Parker and Thane. Rachel slammed shut the microwave door. Robert Thane had offered Rachel's mother money after the death of Marvin Stuart. Blood money, Gail Stuart had called it. Hush money. She'd rejected it and all offers of aid. Dedicated perusal of the Help Wanted ads had landed Mrs. Stuart a job as a department store salesclerk, and twelve-year-old Rachel and her eight-year-old brother, Tony, had assumed many of the household chores. Things once taken for granted such as movies, new clothes and vacation trips became rare and infrequent treats. As teenagers Rachel and Tony held down part-time jobs. Later, jobs, student loans and living at home enabled them to attend a community college.

And all that time Rachel waited for the day she could clear her father's name. All those years wasted. The microwave pinged, jarring her from her self-pity. She couldn't, wouldn't, give up. Only an idiot would expect Nicholas Bonelli to leap at the opportunity to reopen the investigation. He didn't leap. That didn't mean her quest was doomed to failure. Rachel removed the eggs from the oven. "Nicholas Bonelli," she said under her breath, "I've just begun to fight."

Back in the dining area, she slapped the plate of hot eggs and buttered toast on the table near the lakefront windows. "Come eat before you pass out."

Nicholas moved slowly to the table. "You ought to be grateful I turned you down. I could have pretended to investigate and after a suitable length of time told you everything I found pointed to your father's guilt."

She hoped he wasn't waiting for her to thank him. "The coffee should be ready by now." Returning with the pot, she filled a mug for him.

He contemplated the hot, steaming liquid. "If I were soft in the head and undertook your senseless investigation, what makes you think I'd tell you the truth about what I found? In the unlikely event I found evidence that Dad or Thane planted the bid material in your father's office, it would be easy to manipulate the evidence to back up what they said. If my father were dishonest, what makes you think I'd be any more honest?"

"I considered that." Rachel opened the French doors to the screened porch. Lonely wisps of clouds floated across a bleached sky. A barn swallow darted low over the water in ruthless pursuit of bugs, his rust-colored underbelly flashing hunter orange in the fast-rising sun.

"And you decided you could trust me," Nicholas said in a sarcastic voice, "because I'd be so grateful for your Florence Nightingale routine."

"No." A slight morning breeze disturbed her hair. "I decided it didn't matter whether you were honest, because I'd be at your side every step of the way." She turned to face him. "We'd be a team. You, with your knowledge of crime and detection and all that stuff, and me, with my knowledge of my father. And my persistence and determination."

Nicholas stared at her in disbelief, the hand holding his coffee frozen halfway to his mouth. "I cannot begin to imagine any circumstances which would persuade me to allow any client, much less you, to hang over my shoulder as I worked. Your brazen assumptions are exceeded only by your idiotic fantasies."

Lightning flashed across the sky. Through the open windows came the sound of the wind-whipped lake smacking against the huge piles which supported the dock. A mosquito whined past the screened porch. Rachel stared sightlessly at the open book she pretended to read.

The smack of a card against the worn leather surface of the old game table grated on her nerves. Nicholas slapped down another card. He'd been playing solitaire since they'd eaten lunch several hours ago. If Rachel had to listen much longer to the sounds of him continuously shuffling and slapping down cards, she'd go stark raving mad.

He sat in profile to her, providing her with an excellent view of a hollow cheek, jutting chin, and thick blue-black hair. His dark, heavy eyebrow appeared as angry as the scar under his eye. Every square inch of him looked hard, unyielding, tough and rugged. The only halfway civilized body part he owned was a neat, well-shaped ear. It was kind of a cute ear, out of place on Mr. Tough and Macho. He should have a cauliflower ear to go with his cauliflower brain and cauliflower personality. Rachel loathed cauliflower.

A small patch of dark stubble on the side of his jaw pointed out his difficulties in shaving with his left hand. He wasn't having much better luck shuffling one-handed. More than once cards had squirted in all directions. Each time Rachel had silently gathered them up and returned them to him.

He hadn't bothered to thank her.

They'd spoken the barest minimum of words since breakfast, but if Nicholas thought his ringing condemnation of her plan had convinced her to drop it, he was sadly mistaken. At age twelve Rachel had vowed to clear her father. Not until recently had the opportunity to do so come her way. Opportunity in the guise of Nicholas Bonelli.

The cards went flying across the table. When Rachel stood up, Nicholas snapped, "Leave them."

"Tired of losing?"

"Tired of sitting around. Tired of this place. And tired of you staring at me."

She didn't realize he'd noticed. "I'm not—"

"The subject is closed. Finished. *Finito*. The police closed the book on it fifteen years ago, and so should you." He struggled to his feet and stood looking out at the lake. "Not only is there no compelling reason to reopen the investigation, when a detective is emotionally involved, he spends his energies looking for specific evidence to back his favored theory instead of considering all the facts. There's no way I could investigate my own father without bias." He banged the crutch against the floor. "Quit bombarding me with subliminal messages or whatever your staring is supposed to do. It's not working.''

"I wasn't sending messages. It must be your own conscience bothering..." His tightening shoulder muscles warned her away from that minefield. "And I wasn't staring at you. That is, maybe I was, but not because, that is, well... Your ear is cute," she blurted.

Thunder reverberated from the hills beyond the lake. "Don't ever," Nicholas growled, "step in front of my car. If your father was half as obnoxious as you, I wouldn't blame Dad if he did hit the gas pedal.''

Rachel gasped. "And you call me obnoxious.''

"At least I don't go around calling your ears cute.''

"My ears aren't cute. They're too big and stick out.''

He turned slowly and studied her head. "I don't think they're too big.''

"Then they must not be because everyone knows you're a connoisseur of beautiful women," she said in a snippy voice.

"I wouldn't call you beautiful.''

Rachel absorbed the hurtful comment without flinching. "I don't care what you'd call me.''

"Beauty requires a classical face. Yours is interesting.''

"Thank you very much. Next you'll say I'm nice.''

He snorted. "I'm injured, not brain dead. You're a pain in the posterior, but we weren't discussing your personality. We were discussing your face. Oval shape, ivory skin, a few freckles, a small but determined chin, and a too generous mouth add up to interesting.''

Rachel couldn't prevent herself from asking, "Is interesting good or bad? A big mouth sounds bad.''

"In personalities, a big mouth is bad. On a woman's face, a mouth like yours is good. Quit fishing for compliments," he added impatiently. "You must be used to men telling you what a kissable mouth you have.''

She wasn't about to admit she wasn't. "The men I date aren't into superficial judgments."

He raised his brow. "Considering those fruit salad earrings you're wearing, lucky for you."

"Look who's talking. In that yellow sweatsuit you look like an oversized banana."

"At least the top and the bottoms match. I'm not wearing red pants and a blue shirt."

Rachel glared at him. "My slacks aren't red, they're bittersweet." His nasty attitude gave her an excuse for venting pent-up emotion. "And having a boring nature, not to mention a closed mind, is nothing to brag about."

"I suppose having hair like some rodeo clown is."

"You're jealous because my hair is on my head instead of all over my body like some Cro-Magnon relict." She didn't remember crossing the porch floor but she stood toe-to-toe with him, her fists jammed against her hip bones.

"If I were a Cro-Magnon, I'd have bopped you over the head with a club long ago."

"Yeah?" Rachel sneered. "Your mama wears combat boots."

He squinted menacingly at her. "So does your mama."

"She does not. You take that back. You..." The rest of Rachel's words died away as Nicholas exploded with laughter.

"You've been spending too much time on the playground," he managed between gusts of laughter.

"You've been spending too much with crooks and gangsters."

"No," he gasped, "don't start again. I give, I fold, I surrender. You win."

Rachel eyed him with uncertainty. "You're going to investigate for me?"

"Don't be ridiculous. I meant we sounded like five-year-olds, and you proved you could be more childish than I can be.''

"You started it with that crack about my earrings."

"No, you're not dragging me down that path again.'' His amused gaze slid to her ears, then returned to meet her indignant eyes. "I can picture you doing surveillance. You'd probably wear fake handguns for earrings."

"Naturally. What would you expect from a bimbo secretary?"

"You deserved that and worse," Nicholas said heartlessly. "Since we're on the subject of you siccing that kid and his fool dog on me, your feeble attempts at humor fell pathetically flat. There's nothing amusing about using a car as a deadly weapon, pink seat covers or not.''

Rachel rounded her eyes in a blatant display of belated understanding. "I've figured it out. You could have been killed in that accident, and now you're running scared. You're refusing to investigate for me because you're worried I might be a danger to you.'' She gave him a pitying look. "You're safe in my hands."

"If anyone were in danger when you're around, Ms. Stuart, it wouldn't be me."

"Threats, Mr. Bonelli? You and what army? In your condition, you couldn't force a cookie to crum... What? What's the matter?'' Rachel cried as Nicholas swayed. He didn't fall, but it was evident he remained on his feet only through sheer willpower. Dashing to his good side, she kicked aside his crutch and slid under his arm to support him. "Hang on to me, I'll help you to the sofa."

His arm heavy over her shoulders, they staggered across the room. "Can I get you anything?'' Rachel eased him down onto the faded sofa facing the fireplace. "Your pain pills, something to drink? Maybe I should call your doctor."

"No," Nicholas said in a faint voice, "I'm fine.

Maybe a footstool for my leg. Ah, that's better. And my glass of iced tea. Thank you. You might plump up the pillows a little. My leg itches right under the cast. If you could scratch it…to the right, lower, up a little, left, now right, farther right…"

Sitting on his left, Rachel practically laid across Nicholas's lap trying to reach his itch. "How's that?"

He twisted his fingers through her loose-hanging hair. "Just fine, Ms. Stuart. Exactly what I wanted." The strong voice made a mockery of any pain or weakness.

He'd tricked her. For some nefarious purposes of his own, he'd feigned his relapse. "You were faking." Rachel slowly straightened up.

Or tried to. Nicholas's fingers tightened in her hair, forcing her face up to his. "To prove a point."

"That you cheat, lie, and play dirty?"

"I'm not in the etiquette business. And I'm not in the charity business. I'm sorry your dad died when you were young."

"He didn't die. He was—" The little tug on her hair silenced her.

"What your dad did does not reflect on you, so quit wallowing in a past best forgotten and get on with your life. Nothing you do can change what happened or bring your dad back. I'm doing you a kindness by refusing to pander to your fantasy."

"I don't want you to do me any favors."

His fingers tightened in her hair. "I thought a favor was exactly what you want from me."

"I want truth and justice. I'd think you'd want them, too."

Nicholas sighed. "Give it up, Teach. Go back to school where you belong. You're out of your league here. You can't blackmail, threaten or challenge me into doing what you want."

"I wouldn't be so certain of that if I were you."

"No?" He chuckled, his fingers easing their grip on her hair. "You talk tough, but you're soft. Even Ian's dog thinks you're a marshmallow. When you thought I was about to collapse, instead of taking advantage, you practically carried me across the room."

"That had nothing to do with toughness, but with duty. I'm being paid to take care of you."

He grinned. "Admit it. Exploiting my weakness never even occurred to you. You know what your problem is?"

"I'm sure you're dying to tell me."

"You're basically a nice person. Your instincts are for helping, not hurting, people." He studied her face. "You won't go to the newspapers."

"Yes, I will." She forced herself to look steadily into eyes glinting with amusement.

"You're not that kind of person."

"You don't know anything about what kind of person I am."

"A man looks at that mouth of yours and he knows all he needs to know." The amusement faded from his eyes to be replaced with a sensual male awareness as he contemplated her.

The inside of her mouth dried completely up. She couldn't have spoken if she wanted to. Rachel swallowed hard. She couldn't want to kiss a man like Nicholas Bonelli. A man who had more women than she had shoes. A man who mocked red hair and freckles.

A man who set her pulses racing.

The one man in the entire world who wasn't for her. Who never could be. The man whose father had killed her father.

"Let me go," she said, almost in panic.

"Why would I? According to you, we're both stuck up here. A man can only play so much solitaire. And when there's a woman around with a mouth as tempting as yours…''

"You're not the least bit interested in my mouth. You're trying to chase me away.'' Her heart pounded. From helping him across the room. No other reason.

Nicholas uttered a short laugh, but he released her hair and leaned back. "I wonder whether I'm trying to chase you away—'' his gaze never left her face "—or find out how badly you want me to investigate.''

"Not so badly I'd sleep with you.''

"Then you might want to get off my lap.''

Rachel jumped to her feet, knowing her face reflected her embarrassment. He'd never believe she'd been so intent on denying to herself his effect on her, she'd forgotten her compromising position. How could she have forgotten when her body had practically melted into his? She stared down her nose at him. "You can't sidetrack me by calling me nice. You can't scare me away. You can't seduce me.'' Turning on her heel, she walked away before Nicholas could dispute her last statement. Or laugh in her face.

The wake from a passing motorboat undulated slowly to the shore where it lapped gently at the rocks Rachel stood on. The sound of flapping preceded the flight overhead of several gulls, their wings shining white in the midmorning sun. Warmth from the sun heated the outside of Rachel. Inside, a foreboding crept out from her heart to chill every cell in her body. The plan had seemed so easy, so surefire. Meet Nicholas Bonelli, lay out her proposition, and if he didn't immediately agree, threaten to go to the newspapers. Any normal person should have leaped at the opportunity to protect his father's name. But not Nicholas. So convinced his father could do no wrong, he thought her threat laughable.

A swallow darted low over the lake in search of a late

breakfast. She'd already fed Nicholas his. In silence. As she'd served dinner last night. Not because she was pouting, as he charged. Because she was marshaling new arguments to sway him. Or trying to. Her brain seemed to have gone on vacation.

Thanks to Nicholas. He'd confused the issue. It wasn't about him and her. It was about clearing her father's name. Something she'd promised herself and his memory she'd do. Everything had seemed so clear, so black and white. Then Nicholas had pretended he found her attractive. She gave an inelegant snort, startling a mallard floating toward shore. The duck took off with much splashing of water and flapping of wings.

The mallard landed on the water a distance from Rachel. His green head glowed emerald. Naturally a male. His agitated takeoff had fractured the serene blanket of pollen which floated along the shoreline. Messing up Mother Nature's plan. The way Nicholas Bonelli had messed up Rachel's plan.

He'd lied. He didn't find her attractive.

She sat on a large rock and watched the swallow repeat his dives. And wished she didn't find Nicholas attractive. Falling for Nicholas's too obvious charms had not been part of her plan. Not that she was falling. Even if the man would tempt a wooden statue with those brown eyes and that sexy smile. She wasn't the least bit tempted to sleep with him.

No matter how enjoyable the activity might be.

Rachel clasped her hands around her knees and leaned back, closing her eyes in despair. She didn't even like Nicholas Bonelli.

"If you're not pouting, you're scheming."

Rachel almost fell off the rock at the unexpected voice. "Quit sneaking up on me. I'm not pouting."

"Which means you're scheming. When a woman refuses to talk, she's doing one or the other."

"Wisdom from the foremost authority on women, I assume."

"Close enough." He leaned on his crutch. "Save your brain cells. Women's schemes bore me as much as pouting does. You may as well admit failure right now."

Rachel squared her shoulders and gave him a disdainful look. "I wasn't brought up to admit failure. Unlike some, I was raised to fight."

"With that red hair, I'll bet you were a little hellraiser."

Rachel dug her fingernails into her knees. He wielded patronizing remarks as weapons to render her harmless. She wouldn't let him succeed. "I still can be a hellraiser."

A hummingbird whistled past in the stark silence following her words. The swallow dove for another insect.

Nicholas uttered a quiet laugh devoid of amusement. "I used to pride myself on being able to read people. You, Teach, have taught me I need a class in remedial reading. I wouldn't have thought you'd sink so low."

Rachel raised her chin and stared determinedly at the lake. She wouldn't let him beat her down. "I told you clearing my father is important to me."

"If he's innocent, he'd be proud of your methods, wouldn't he?"

She blinked. "He's innocent, and he'd be proud of me doing what I have to do."

"Is your mother proud, too? And your brother?"

"I haven't discussed this with them," Rachel said carefully. She hadn't wanted to get their hopes up.

"I'm happy to hear that. I'd hate to think a mother would encourage her daughter to barter her body. Forget it. I'm withdrawing the offer. I have no interest in sleeping with you."

Rachel sprang to her feet and faced him. "Sleep with

me? I'm not going to sleep with you.'' Comprehension dawned. ''I meant I'd go to the newspapers.''

''That doesn't worry me.''

So easily he dismissed her most potent threat. She wanted to poke him with her little finger and knock him over. Instead she gave him a provocative look. ''But I do? Interesting.''

''I didn't say that.''

She walked two fingers up his uninjured arm. ''Is the big bad man afraid of little Rachel?'' She thrust out her bottom lip. ''Is little Nicky afraid I'll seduce him into doing what I want him to do?''

He stood stone-faced, looking down at her. Only the darkening of his eyes hinted at his annoyance. ''My body may be weakened by my injuries, but my brain isn't. Your pathetic attempts to seduce me are laughable. I'm not interested in a criminal's daughter who's neurotic, a bad dresser and an all-around pain in the neck.''

Rachel spun around and walked a few steps away. Her hands clenched at her sides, she faced the lake. The swallow dive-bombed for another bug and landed on the water. ''Well,'' she said with determined brightness, watching the bird paddle on the water, ''that takes care of that issue, doesn't it?''

Gravel crunched as Nicholas made his way to her side. The swallow beat his wings at the water. Rachel watched the bird and ignored Nicholas. He'd said more than enough already.

''Maybe my injuries have weakened my brain,'' Nicholas said. ''I'm not usually rude to women.''

''Only to criminals' daughters,'' Rachel flung.

Nicholas inhaled deeply. ''If you want me to apologize—''

''I only want one thing from you. The truth about my father.'' She frowned. ''Nicholas, I don't think the swallow can get off the water. He's getting exhausted from trying." She stepped tentatively into the water.

"What are you doing? I'm trying to apologize here."

"Fine." The stones were slippery beneath her feet. "The water seems to be bringing him this way. Maybe I can reach him."

"My mother has a lot to answer for, sticking me up here with a lunatic like you. Here." Nicholas thrust his crutch at her. "Try bringing him closer with this."

The swallow paid no attention to the stick coming at him. Rachel gingerly guided the sodden bundle of feathers toward her. Back on dry land, Rachel dropped the crutch and scooped up the small bird. It huddled miserably in her cupped palms. "Now what?"

"Put him in a sheltered place where he can dry off and rest. He'll be fine."

Rachel set the bird in the lee of a large boulder and slowly backed away. The bird gave her an unblinking stare. Picking up Nicholas's crutch, she handed it to him. "Thank you."

"You're welcome. Just out of curiosity, how far out did you plan to go?"

"I hoped I wouldn't have to go any deeper than my knees." Rachel slowed her pace to accommodate Nicholas. "My neurosis, you know."

Nicholas halted. "I tried to apologize."

"For what? Saying out loud what you think? I don't care what you think, Nicholas Bonelli. I'm going to clear my father's name, with or without your help. If that makes me a pain in the neck, good. And if you were the hotshot detective you think you are, you'd know I don't give one big fat darn whether you like how I dress or not." She wheeled around and headed for the house. A swift-moving crutch came from behind her to bar her way.

"If I were a hotshot detective—" Nicholas pulled her

back to where he stood "—I'd figure out what it is about you that makes me want to do this.''

She couldn't shove him. Not with his battered body. Gingerly she placed her right hand against the left side of his chest to restrain him. Her hand provided no barrier at all.

Nicholas slanted his mouth warmly across hers.

Rachel promptly forgot she disliked him. Forgot she shouldn't be kissing him. She forgot everything except the taste, the feel, the heat of Nicholas's mouth.

She'd never been kissed like this before. Excitement simmered and sizzled through her veins. His heart thudded against her palm, each quickening beat sending an incandescent charge up her arm. Her hand curled, crushing his shirt between her fingers. At his urging, her lips parted. Excitement shot to the pit of her stomach as Nicholas slowly, intimately, acquainted himself with the moist recesses of her mouth. Pleasure broke over her in waves.

Nicholas curled his good hand around the nape of her neck, pulling her closer. Every square inch of Rachel's body felt gloriously alive, and she responded enthusiastically. Greedy for more of the bliss his mouth introduced her to, she threw both arms around his neck and pulled herself up on her tiptoes.

Nicholas made a sharp sound and broke off the kiss.

Awareness flooded back. Rachel dropped her arms and stared at his chest. How to explain insanity? She didn't want to kiss this man. She wanted to use him.

Her rapid, shallow breathing sounded deafening in her ears. He couldn't help but hear it. "I'm sorry. I don't know what got into me." She thought of his deep kisses and felt the fiery blush climb up her face at the unhappy choice of words.

"You're a dangerous woman."

"I'm sorry," she said again, apologizing to his chest. "I didn't mean to hurt your shoulder."

"I wasn't talking about my shoulder. A woman who wears a blue cow necklace shouldn't be allowed to kiss like that."

She couldn't possibly ask like what, so she responded to the other part of his sentence. "I wear this kind of jewelry because I teach first grade, and bright, fun jewelry focuses the children's attention so they listen better to what I'm saying."

"I should have known you were dangerous the minute I saw your mouth. Your kind of mouth always spells trouble." Nicholas tapped his crutch on a small boulder. "I admit there's some kind of chemical attraction between us. In all honesty, you would worry me. If you were the type of woman willing to barter her body to get what she wanted."

A myriad of confusing, contradictory thoughts muddled Rachel's mind. She didn't want to like Nicholas. She didn't want to be aware of him as a man. She wanted to throw herself back in his arms. "What if I were?" she asked slowly. "You're wrong about a lot of things about me. Maybe you're wrong about that, too. Maybe I am."

His gaze never faltered. "In that case, Teach," he said flatly, "we're both in trouble."

CHAPTER FIVE

RACHEL spread strawberry jam on a slice of bread. What kind of man ate peanut butter and jam and banana sandwiches? She stared vacantly out the window over the sink. The kind of man who kissed a woman stupid and then pretended he couldn't help himself. Who blamed the kiss on chemical attraction. She smashed the two slices of bread together and cut the sandwich into four triangles. Nicholas hated sandwiches cut into little triangles. He called them sissy sandwiches. What did he think peanut butter and jam and banana sandwiches were? Macho meals?

Not that she cared. Any more than she cared he was trying to drive her away by pretending a chemical reaction bigger than both of them. He must think first-grade teachers were as naive as their six-year-old students. Half his body parts were injured and inoperable, which ruled out physical intimidation, so he was playing mind games. Trying to frighten her with her own reaction to his kisses. He couldn't. She'd be worried if she hadn't reacted. Kissing women stupid was his stock-in-trade.

He probably expected her to run for home. Which undoubtedly explained his annoying grouchiness ever since he'd kissed her. He was going to get a whole lot grouchier, because she had no intention of leaving. Not until he agreed to investigate. When Rachel Stuart wanted something, she personified water wearing down stone.

The phone rang as she set the sandwich on the table

in front of Nicholas. Ignoring the look of disgust he gave his mangled lunch, she crossed to answer the phone.

"If you've killed him," Dyan said without preamble, "dump his body in Lake Granby. It's bigger than Grand Lake and deeper than Shadow Mountain Reservoir."

Rachel laughed. "He's been good as gold," she said, knowing full well Nicholas could hear her.

"You whacked him over the head with the fireplace poker, didn't you?"

"He's right here. You can talk to him." Rachel carried the phone over to Nicholas.

He scowled at her and the receiver. "Who is it?"

"Dyan."

"Tell my loving sister I have nothing to say to her until she gets her sorry self up here to apologize for her dirty trick and to take me home."

"Forget it." Dyan's voice came clearly over the wires.

At the sour look on Nicholas's face, Rachel moved the phone out of his reach before he yanked the wire from the wall.

"I warned you he's impossible," Dyan said in Rachel's ear. "I'll find someone else to be his lackey if you can't stand him any longer."

"No, everything's fine," Rachel said quickly. The last thing she wanted was to be replaced. "If he's a little crabby at times, I don't mind. I know he's in pain."

"No," Dyan howled. "Don't tell me you're falling for him."

"Of course not."

"He's a piranha and you're a little guppy. Oh, Rachel, what have I done to you? I never thought you and him... When you were little did you have underpants with the days of the week embroidered on them?"

"Yes, but what—"

"Nick has days-of-the-week women. I mean, I dearly

love my big brother, and I know he's considered a hunk, but I'm not blind to his faults. He can't commit. You're meant to be a wife and mother, not a decoration on Nick's arm every other Sunday at 2:00 p.m. or whenever he can fit you into his social schedule. Trust me, Rachel, Nick isn't your type. You're sweet and kind and generous and—oh, darn and double darn. It's your red hair."

"What on earth are you talking about?"

"He's dated blondes and brunettes and women with black hair and sun-streaked hair and probably even gray hair, but I don't think he's ever dated a redhead. Why didn't I think of that? If he hasn't driven you to murder, then he's putting moves on you. I could shoot myself for getting you into this."

"You didn't get me into anything," Rachel said firmly. "You might give me a little credit. I can take care of myself."

"When Nick sets his sights on a woman, she's a goner."

"What does a man have to do to get something to drink with his lunch?" Nicholas bellowed from the table.

"Dyan, I have to go." Conscious of Nicholas openly listening to her conversation, Rachel carefully chose her words. "Don't worry. Everything's fine." Behind her, Nicholas growled something. "Gotta go. 'Bye." Rachel hung up on Dyan's sputtered questions.

Nicholas leaned back against his chair. "You ought to listen to Dyan."

How did he know what she'd said? Rachel deliberately misunderstood him. "And dump your body in Lake Granby? Considering how I feel about boats and water, how am I supposed to get you there?"

"She warned you away from me, didn't she?"

"A warning I have no need of since I have no personal interest in you. All I want from you are your detecting skills.''

"Did you think they're contagious, that you can get them by kissing me?''

"You kissed me.''

"And you kissed me back. Willingly.''

Never back down, a veteran teacher told her. Never let them think they have the upper hand. "And I thoroughly enjoyed myself. You're an excellent kisser. I'll give you an A-plus on that kiss.''

"I'll give you a D-minus.''

"You need something to drink. A nice glass of cold milk.''

"I want a cola.''

"Milk mends bones.''

"Suppose I said a D-minus due to lack of experience, but considering the enthusiasm you put into the kiss, I might raise your grade to, say, a B-plus?''

She ignored the blush heating her cheeks. "You'd still get milk. Carbonation interferes with bones absorbing calcium or vitamin D or something.''

"Do not make the mistake of thinking you have the upper hand here. When I ask for a glass of cola, I want a glass of cola.'' He rubbed his shoulder. "Is that clear?''

Contrition brought her up short. "Is your shoulder hurting?'' she asked sympathetically.

"Don't patronize me. I am not one of your students.'' He was definitely spoiling for a fight.

"If you were, I'd have sent you to the principal's office long ago.'' Rachel couldn't remember the last time she'd sent a child from the room for behavior she couldn't deal with. "But you're a grumpy adult male who's too macho to admit he's in pain, so you're taking your bad temper out on me.''

"You can leave anytime, Ms. Stuart.''

"Fat chance, Mr. Bonelli." She went to the kitchen for his drink. Returning, she said, "If you want to get rid of me, investigate the crime my father was framed for."

"Fat chance." He snarled her remark back at her.

"*Bon appétit.*" She slammed the glass down in front of him. The ringing doorbell doubtlessly saved her from a faceful of cold milk.

Ian grinned at her from the front stoop. "Hi, Rachel."

"Hi." Rachel looked down at the slightly smaller, slightly chubbier version of Ian giving her a gaping-tooth grin. "You must be Ian's brother, Eric."

"See, she knows who you are and I didn't tell her," Ian said triumphantly. "I told ya Nick and Dollface are detectives." He gave his brother a minatory frown. "You hafta call her Rachel. Nick calls her Dollface cuz she's his, you know, like on TV. She's his bean, bin... What did Nick say you are, Rachel?" he innocently appealed. "His what?"

"Bimbo secretary." There was no hope Nicholas wasn't listening to every word of this conversation. Rachel heard him moving from the table. "What's up? Don't tell me your disreputable, conniving canine pal took off for parts unknown again."

A puzzled frown wrinkled Ian's brow for a moment. "Oh, you mean Scotty. No, I got us another case," he said proudly. "Molly's got a problem. We gotta see Nick." He shoved a small girl forward.

Rachel hadn't noticed the child hiding behind Ian. She placed the girl's age at about five. "Hello, Molly."

The girl gave Rachel a quick, doubtful glance from under lowered eyelids.

"Need a detective," Eric piped up. "Crystal's gone."

The little girl's mouth wobbled and her brown eyes filled with tears.

"Eric!" Ian hollered. "You big dummy! Now she's

gonna cry again. I oughta make you stay out here with Scotty.''

"Scotty?" The gangling puppy raced around the corner of the house toward Rachel, woofing loudly with delight. Unable to put on his brakes in time, Scotty slid across the stoop toward her. The way the three children scattered from his path told Rachel they'd had plenty of practice evading a dog who enjoyed romps in the lake.

Rachel removed two huge muddy paws from her shoulders. "Get down." Obedient for once, the dog dropped to all fours and shook vigorously. Cold, smelly lake water rained over Rachel. Giving her a canine grin as she wiped the water from her face, Scotty detoured around her, his tail flying high. He trotted into the living room in the children's wake.

"Don't say a word," Rachel said, following the dog.

Nicholas's mouth barely twitched. "The two of you give new meaning to the phrase 'teacher's pet.' It must have something to do with your strict discipline.'' He glanced at the dog laying calmly and obediently near his chair, before turning to Ian. "What's this about a case? I thought I explained I'm on convalescent leave of absence from being a detective.''

Ian nodded. "I know, Nick, but this is an emergency." The three children stood at Nicholas's elbow, impatient to begin.

Nicholas tensed. "What kind of emergency?"

Remembering Nicholas rubbing his shoulder, Rachel might have discouraged the children's plans for hauling him on another animal hunt. If she hadn't spotted the wicked amusement in his eyes when he'd seen the muddy footprints and wet splotches decorating her blouse and slacks. "Your services as a hotshot detective are in demand again. Ian brought you a new client. This is Molly and her dog is gone.''

The children looked at Rachel as if she'd lost her mind.

"Molly ain't gotta dog," Eric said.

"She's her sister," Ian said at the same time.

"Whoa, wait a minute," Nicholas said. "Hello, Molly." He smiled at the small girl.

She returned a shy, sweet smile. "Does it hurt bad?" Concern filled her voice.

Rachel shook her head. All the man had to do was look at a female and she handed him her heart. Except Rachel, of course.

"Sometimes," Nicholas answered Molly, "but it's better now the three of you have come to visit."

Adoration blazed from two pairs of blue eyes and one pair of brown. Two pairs of brown eyes if Rachel counted the dog.

"Rachel said you had a problem."

"It's her sister. Tell Nick." Ian prodded the little girl with his hand. "He can find anybody."

"Crystal's gone," Molly said obediently. "We was playing wif paper dolls and I hadda take a nap and when I got up she was gone and Mama keeps crying and saying Crystal's gone and I want her back but Mama says she's gone and she didn't say goodbye so I know she's not gone but I can't find her and I want her back and I want Mama to quit crying." The flow of words stopped and a small tear trailed down Molly's cheek.

"Oh, boy," Nicholas said softly.

"Don't cry, Molly." Ian awkwardly patted the little girl's back. "Nick will fix it."

The little girl sniffed and stared hopefully up at Nicholas.

"Oh, boy," Nicholas said again. He gave Rachel a look of appeal. "Any ideas?"

All else fled in the face of the child's distress. "Why don't we have some cookies while you plan strategy?"

She didn't bother to analyze her assumption that Nicholas would solve Molly's problem.

"Let Molly and Eric help you."

"I could use help. No, Scotty, not you," Rachel said firmly. "I will not have you in the kitchen. All right, all right, but if you must be in here, you have to behave yourself. Eric, remove his paws from the countertop."

By the time Rachel had shoved the dog from the kitchen twice and shut both doors, supervised hand-washing, poured five glasses of milk, filled a plate with cookies, and led her helpers out to the screened porch, Ian was returning the telephone to its resting place under the stairs.

Nicholas followed them to the porch. "I talked to Ian's mom," he murmured to Rachel. To the kids, he said, "Eat first. I can't investigate without cookies." He raised his eyebrows at the glass of milk Rachel handed him, but said nothing to her, instead asking Eric about his birthday party.

His remembering such a small detail amazed Rachel until she reminded herself detectives made their living ferreting out and keeping track of minutia. It didn't surprise her when Eric and Molly, who'd been at the birthday party, practically tripped over their words and each other in their eagerness to supply Nicholas with details about the festivities. Nicholas definitely had a way with children. She glanced at Scotty laying at Nicholas's feet. And a way with dogs. He'd make a great father. An image of her holding a brown-eyed baby flashed through her mind, startling her. Shaken, she looked thankfully at Ian as he edged near.

"Nick says hotshot detectives like him don't in tear, uh..." He screwed up his face.

"Interrogate?" Rachel suggested.

"Yeah. They don't do that to little kids. Just big kids like me. Nick don't like girls crying. Not that he don't like Molly," Ian hurriedly assured Rachel, "just it makes him feel bad. Nick said we gotta take care of kids littler than us."

Rachel glanced across to where Molly basked under Nicholas's full attention. "I see."

Ian twisted his mouth in disgust. "Nick says I gotta take 'em down by the lake so he can talk to you. He don't want Molly crying again."

Shortly thereafter the trio of children and one large puppy trailed down to the lake. Rachel stationed herself where she could keep an eye on them.

"Don't worry about them. It's shallow there," Nick said. "If one did fall in, he'd be better at rescuing you than you'd be at rescuing any of them," he added in a matter-of-fact voice.

Rachel decided to let the comment pass. "Ian said you called his mom. What did Mrs. McDonnell have to say?"

"Molly's mom left Molly with Mrs. McDonnell for the afternoon. Ian told his mom they were coming over here to talk to me." He grimaced. "Mrs. McDonnell said he's got a bad case of hero worship. I suspect she thought they'd entertain the invalid. She knew nothing of their agenda."

"Does she know about Crystal?"

"Mrs. McDonnell agrees Crystal seems to be missing, but said although she occasionally watches Molly, she and Molly's mom aren't close so she hasn't asked where Crystal is. Molly's five and Crystal is fourteen. In spite of the age difference, apparently the two girls are very close. Ian's mom said a person would never guess the girls are supposed to be sisters. The emphasis on 'supposed to be' is Mrs. McDonnell's."

"Do you think," Rachel asked slowly, "the two aren't really sisters? That's why Crystal left?"

"Don't jump to conclusions. I told Mrs. McDonnell

the kids could stay here until Molly's mom gets back. I'll talk to her. Let's go out on the deck before Ian gets too impatient. He wants me to strap on a .44 Magnum and rush over to Molly's house. He's convinced Crystal has been kidnapped and the kidnappers have threatened to kill her if her mom talks. I'll try to subtly dig up more information from Molly.''

''But not interrogate her?''

''Hell, no. I hate it when females cry.''

''I know. Ian told me.''

The dog beat the children to the deck. Scotty calmly acknowledged Nicholas before going into a frenzied paroxysm of delight at the sight of Rachel. Heaving a long-suffering sigh, she went into the house to find a broom to sweep up the pieces of the cookie plate.

With her short, light-brown ringlets and huge brown eyes, Molly's mom was a grown-up version of her daughter. Sharie Carter even wore the same expression of half adoration, half appeal on her heart-shaped face as she gazed at Nicholas.

Trying not to compare her dog-splattered pumpkin trousers with Sharie's spotless pink shorts, Rachel watched from the porch as the children threw sticks into the lake for Scotty to retrieve. And shamelessly eavesdropped.

Sharie had pulled one of the wicker chairs on the porch close to where Nicholas sat on the daybed. So the children wouldn't hear their conversation, she'd explained. Much closer and she'd be sprawled in Nicholas's lap. He didn't look as if he'd mind. The memory of herself sprawled across Nicholas flashed across Rachel's mind, and she heard the echo of Dyan's voice saying Nicholas had women for every day of the week. No doubt Nicholas was auditioning Sharie Carter to fill the slot for a woman at the lake. Rachel certainly didn't want the role.

"I don't know how to tell Molly," Sharie was saying. "Crystal's so dear to me, sometimes I forget she's not my daughter." She wiped away a tear with the back of her hand. "My husband was married before. I was his secretary."

Rachel's eyes flew to Nicholas's face to see if the words "bimbo secretary" popped into his mind. He was busy murmuring soothing platitudes to Sharie.

"Tom's first wife was an alcoholic, and when they divorced, he got custody of Crystal," Sharie went on. "Not long after that, Crystal's mom died. After Molly was born, Tom decided he wanted the kids to grow up in a small town so he bought the house and moved us up here. Since his business is in Denver, he only came up weekends."

She managed a trembling smile. "I should have suspected he was running around. I was pregnant when he divorced his first wife. We've been divorced three years. Tom never wanted the responsibilities of marriage or fatherhood. He left Crystal with me." She dabbed her eyes. "He remarried in January and his wife had a baby in May. She's high society, tall, blond, rich. He doesn't mind fatherhood with her."

Even on the screened porch, the heavy scent of Sharie's perfume gave Rachel a headache. It had obviously poisoned Nicholas's brain. Despite his earlier claim, he didn't seem to mind Sharie's tears. Not many women could cry without their eyes turning red and puffy and their noses dripping. Sharie Carter's makeup didn't even run.

More tears flowed down the woman's lovely face. "Tom and the money and the Denver house and a baby weren't enough. Brittany had to have Crystal. She didn't want Molly." Sharie sniffled. "Said she couldn't deal with a small child and a baby at the same time. What Brittany wanted was a baby-sitter." Sharie wiped her eyes again. "How could I tell Molly her daddy wanted Crystal but not her?"

"It must be very difficult for you, Mrs. Carter."

Difficult for her? What about Molly? And Crystal? Rachel wanted to smack Sharie. Right after she smacked Nicholas.

"Call me Sharie. Surely I can call you Nick since the children do." She blinked tear-drenched eyes and smiled shyly. "I can tell that Molly already idolizes you. She needs a man in her life. Tom hardly ever bothers with her."

"Molly's lucky to have a mother like you," Nicholas said. "It's obvious you care a great deal for Crystal, too."

"I do, I do." Sharie brushed wet eyelashes. "But I don't have custody of Crystal, so there wasn't anything I could do. Was there?"

"I'm afraid I don't know anything about custody. Have you talked to a lawyer?"

Sharie pouted. "I'm not very good with lawyers. They're always telling me I can't do what I want. I thought a person hired lawyers so she could do what she wanted. Mrs. McDonnell said you're a private detective. I thought you could help me."

"I'm sorry, Sharie. I'm not that kind of detective. I wish I could help you, but our firm does criminal investigations for corporations."

"I don't know what to do." Sharie's eyes welled up again. "You must think I'm such a crybaby, Nick. Thank you for listening to my problems. Being a woman alone is so hard. It helps to have a man's advice."

Rachel had yet to hear one bit of advice, good, bad or indifferent come from Nicholas Bonelli's mouth. This was supposed to be about Molly. Not about Sharie Carter needing a man for her bedroom. Grabbing a box of paper tissues, Rachel stuck it in Sharie's face and took charge of the conversation. "Will Crystal be coming back?"

"I don't know." Sharie blew her nose. "I'm afraid to ask."

Rachel managed to avoid rolling her eyes. Antagonizing Sharie wouldn't help Molly. "You need to discuss this with your ex-husband. How did Crystal feel about going to Denver?"

"Excited, what with the new baby, and shopping malls and everything. Maybe she won't want to come back. What can I tell Molly?" Sharie moaned.

"The truth. She needs to know Crystal didn't run away or disappear. If you don't give Molly an explanation," Rachel added, "she's liable to imagine something horrible. It might help Molly if she could phone Crystal occasionally. Everything must be strange and bewildering to Crystal, too. She may be fourteen, but she's had it rough, losing her mother. She may think you wanted to get rid of her."

Sharie gave Rachel a horrified look. "I love Crystal."

To her surprise, Rachel believed the woman. Her voice warmed slightly. "I'm sure Crystal knows that, and I'm sure she loves you. Even if she decides to stay in Denver, or your husband decides she's better off there, because of schools or something," Rachel added carefully, "Molly and Crystal will always be sisters, so you'll always be a part of her life."

"Rachel's right, Sharie. There are ways of telling Molly the truth without letting her know she wasn't wanted. If you let Molly go on thinking Crystal disappeared, eventually Molly will start worrying you're going to disappear, too."

"I don't know how to tell her without crying."

"That's okay," Nicholas said in a gentle tone. "It's

an honest emotion. Molly misses Crystal and she'd expect you to miss her, too.''

Sharie gave him a wide-eyed, worshiping look. "Oh, Nick, you don't know how much good it's done me to discuss this with you. A man can look at a problem and see immediately how to solve it. Thank you so much.''

Rachel stared determinedly out at the lake. A crow flew over the water calling raucously. In the distance another crow answered. Sharie continued to effusively thank Nicholas for his help and support and advice. The children laughed and shouted as they threw another stick and Scotty plunged into the water after it. From up on the porch Rachel heard the dog panting. Unless that was Nicholas she heard panting. He'd better not expect Rachel to chauffeur him back and forth to any assignations.

Several hours later Sharie finally departed, taking with her the three children and the dog.

Rachel couldn't decide whom she was happier to see leave, Scotty, who slobbered his farewell all over her trousers, or Sharie Carter, who slobbered her gratitude all over Nicholas.

Not that Nicholas making another conquest bothered Rachel. She wasn't jealous of the warm smiles he gave Sharie, merely saddened by the way women like Sharie simpered over men like Nicholas. Dark brown eyes, wavy blue-black hair and six feet of sex appeal weren't such a big deal. If Sharie needed a man in her life so badly, she should contact a dating service.

The door closed more sharply than Rachel intended.

Nicholas stood in the living room when she came down the hall. He gave her a quizzical look. "The wind blew the door out of my hands,'' she said defensively. "I didn't mean to slam it.''

"Who were you giving the bum's rush to? Scotty or Sharie?''

"I doubt if Scotty would be discouraged if I slammed his entire head in the door."

"So you wanted to discourage Sharie."

"Of course not." Leave it to Nicholas to come up with the one scenario which was definitely not true. Next he'd accuse her of being jealous of Sharie Carter. "Sharie's perfectly charming, but I can't believe she didn't ask when or if Crystal was coming back. Poor Crystal probably thought she was being kicked out. And poor Molly, not to be told the truth."

"Sharie's doing the best she knows how to do. It isn't her fault all the rules are being rewritten these days."

"How typical of a man. Sharie's cute and clingy, so you turn into Sir Galahad. I'm surprised you didn't offer to take your .45 Magnum down to Denver and blow her ex-husband away."

"It's a .44 Magnum, and I don't own one."

"You said Ian wanted you to take your whatever Magnum over to rescue Crystal. Never mind," she added quickly as he opened his mouth, "you know what I mean."

"I certainly do. Sharie isn't willing to blackmail me or threaten me or sleep with me to get me to investigate her ex-husband, so you think she's weak."

Rachel's initial reaction was relief that his conclusion was so far from what she'd expected. Her second was that he must think constant repetition of his offer to investigate in exchange for sleeping with her would scare her off or maneuver her into his bed. A third thought thrust its way into her head. Nicholas had made his proposal, positive it would send her packing. When it hadn't, he'd started worrying she'd take him up on his offer. The conviction took hold of Rachel that he would no more barter his services for sex than she would.

She gave him a pitying look. "Sharie Carter has a history of sleeping with a man to get what she wants.

She admitted she slept with her boss, and they got married because she was pregnant.'' Rachel smirked at him. "Don't lose hope. She's probably sitting at home right now figuring out the logistics of sleeping with a man who's wrapped from head to toe in plaster.''

"Fiberglass,'' Nicholas said. "Don't worry, Teach, when you leave, it won't be because Sharie's replacing you.''

"I'm not worried. She's not looking for a job. She's looking for a new boyfriend.'' And Rachel couldn't care less.

Nicholas shook his head. "She's looking for a husband and a father for Molly, but she'll have to search elsewhere. Marriage isn't on my program.''

"With Bunny and Summer and Tiffany and all the rest of them on standby, I can understand how it would be a sacrifice to settle down with one woman.''

"You keep harping on the women in my life, as if I'm hurting or deceiving them in some way, but I'm dating more than one woman so they all know right up front our relationship comes with no strings, no promises and no commitments,'' he said evenly. "You advised Sharie to tell the truth. I tell the truth, and no woman has expectations or gets hurt.''

"Oh, please. I've taught school too long to be fooled by a bratty kid trying to convince me a purely selfish behavior is actually altruistic.'' She widened her eyes in a parody of innocence. "Gosh, Ms. Stuart, I really thought Sissy would love a handful of worms in her pocket.''

He gave a short laugh. "Marriage to me would definitely be worse than worms in a woman's pocket.''

"Let me guess. You tell every woman your job's so dangerous it wouldn't be fair to marry her only to make her a widow.''

"I do not—''

Rachel cut off his indignant denial. "It's bad enough to try and fool other people. Don't lie to yourself. Your job's not that dangerous. You're dealing with white-collar criminals, not murderers and thugs."

"James Donet embezzled a million dollars. If that doesn't make him a thug, smashing me with his car does."

"One time a crook gets carried away. You know very well you're using your job as an excuse to avoid commitment."

"I don't know who told you that, but it wasn't Dyan."

"It certainly was. She said you were incapable of committing."

"She's right."

"I wouldn't brag about it, if I were you."

"How old did you say you are, Ms. Stuart?"

"That has nothing to do with—"

"Thirty? Thirty-five?"

"Twenty-seven," she snapped. His grin told her she'd fallen into his trap. "My age is irrelevant."

"Are you engaged to be married?"

"What does—"

"Have a significant other?"

"I don't see—"

"Dating anyone special?"

"It's none of—"

"What's the matter? Don't believe in marriage? Have trouble committing?"

"I have every intention of getting married and having a family. I simply haven't found the right man. When I get married, it will be forever. I want a love like my mother and father had."

"So did I," Nicholas said unexpectedly.

"Did? I didn't know you'd, that is..." Sorry she'd pushed the subject, Rachel fumbled for words. "Dyan never said, are you divorced?"

"I never got that lucky. If I were divorced, at least I would have been in love once."

Rachel frowned at the regret—or was it self-pity?—in his voice. "It's not like you're too old to fall in love."

"You don't know? I'm surprised Dyan didn't tell you. I'm the odd man out in my family. The object of everyone's else's pity. Poor ole Nick—he can't fall in love."

"Everyone can fall in love."

"My family has a long-standing tradition of falling hard and fast at a very early age. My great-grandparents married when she was seventeen and he was nineteen."

"Your rich grandparents?"

"He was rich, the son of a railroad magnate. She was a housemaid. Their daughter, my grandmother, eloped at age eighteen with the family gardener during World War II. Grandfather Kimbell died at sea, and Grandmother moved back into the family mansion in Chicago with her parents. My mom and dad fell in love in high school in Chicago. They eloped in the teeth of family opposition when Mom was nineteen."

"Because she was so young?"

"Because Grandad Bonelli ran a neighborhood grocery store."

"The housemaid and the gardener's wife objected?" Rachel asked incredulously.

"Grandmother Kimbell said later if it was meant to be, love would find a way."

"So it was sort of a test."

"Grandmother had no intention of being estranged from her only child," Nicholas said dryly. "She chose what she considered to be the philosophical high road. My dad says the old bat just couldn't admit she'd been wrong about him."

Rachel refused to be diverted by a family joke. "I don't see what any of that has to do with your refusal to commit."

"I'm telling you. Family tradition."

She gave him a skeptical look. "Are you telling me you can't get married until you find some poor woman who does not run in the same rarefied social circles you run in? That's ridiculous. Dyan married Charles Addison, and his family's rolling in dough. Dyan and Charlie have a terrific marriage."

"At age sixteen, Dyan took one look at Charlie and never looked elsewhere. Dad said Charlie was a spoiled brat and a playboy who'd never amount to anything. Dyan was deaf to Dad's objections. They married on her nineteenth birthday, carrying on the family tradition. Love comes early to my family. You can trace the family tree, any limb, and every single person who married happily, married young."

"Are you claiming it's too late for you to get married?"

Nicholas fiddled with his shoulder brace. "I've told myself it's a silly superstition, but when you've been brought up on family lore which insists to have a happy marriage in our family you have to fall in love early, and with someone your parents object to, it's difficult to view the matter logically."

"That is the stupidest thing I've ever heard."

"You think I don't know that?" He leaned his head back on the sofa cushions and closed his eyes. "I started waiting to fall in love when I was fifteen. I expected to be in love and engaged, if not married, when I graduated from college, but I didn't worry until I hit age twenty-five, and my family started looking at me askance and asking questions. Mom hauled out the daughters of her friends. Dad trotted out daughters of co-workers and acquaintances. Dyan brought home sorority sisters. Even Charlie got in on the act, wanting to hire women on the basis of their qualifications for marriage rather than qualifications for employment."

He shook his head. "You wouldn't believe how many beautiful, eligible women they paraded past me. Bright, funny, clever, intelligent women. I liked most of them. I didn't fall in love with any of them."

"Of course you didn't. Have you ever seen a kid in a candy store? His mom tells him to pick something out, and he can't. If he starts to take a peppermint stick, he thinks a sucker might be better. Or bubble gum, or a chocolate candy bar. He has too many choices. You have a dozen women. No one woman could possibly hope to be all of them."

"Getting married isn't the same as buying a piece of candy. A man doesn't pick out a wife. He falls in love." Nicholas opened his eyes and gazed steadily at Rachel. "And the simple truth is, I'm incapable of falling in love."

The Editor's "Thank You" Free Gifts Include:

- Two BRAND-NEW romance novels!
- An exciting mystery gift!

PLACE
FREE GIFT
SEAL
HERE

YES! I have placed my Editor's "Thank You" seal in the space provided above. Please send me 2 free books and an exciting mystery gift. I understand I am under no obligation to purchase any books, as explained on the back and on the opposite page.

116 HDL CF29 (U-H-R-03/98)

Name

Address   Apt.

City

State   Zip

Thank You!

DETACH AND MAIL CARD TODAY!

Harlequin Reader Service® – Here's How It Works:

If offer card is missing write to: Harlequin Reader Service, 3010 Walden Ave., P.O. Box 1867, Buffalo, NY 14240-1867

BUSINESS REPLY MAIL
FIRST-CLASS MAIL   PERMIT NO. 717   BUFFALO, NY

POSTAGE WILL BE PAID BY ADDRESSEE

HARLEQUIN READER SERVICE
3010 WALDEN AVE
PO BOX 1867
BUFFALO NY 14240-9952

NO POSTAGE
NECESSARY
IF MAILED
IN THE
UNITED STATES

CHAPTER SIX

"ONLY an idiot would believe something so preposterous."

Nicholas reached for his crutch and pulled himself to his feet. "I had you believing me for a while, didn't I? You're such a bleeding heart, I thought it would be fun to pull your leg." He went out to the screened porch, pulling shut the French doors behind him. Making it very clear he wanted no company.

She eyed him through the glass-paned doors uncomfortably aware of a sudden, sinking feeling deep in the pit of her stomach. What if Nicholas hadn't been pulling her leg but had been sharing his innermost conviction? If there was one thing she detested, it was a teacher's failure to treat a child's feelings with care and delicacy. Feelings couldn't be right or wrong. She didn't believe in telling a child he should or shouldn't feel a certain way. Yet she'd treated Nicholas's revelations with all the delicacy and finesse of a platoon of boot-clad moose marching through a strawberry patch.

Irritation swept over her. Talk about delusional. He'd been playing on her sympathies, and she'd almost fallen for it. Instead of tracking down crooks, Nicholas Bonelli ought to be giving lessons on how to deceive unsuspecting victims.

It wasn't as if one needed a gene which predisposed one to falling in love. How gullible did he think she was? Next he would have claimed he couldn't fall in love because of flawed DNA or something equally absurd.

Even more absurd was the idea of Nicholas Bonelli

baring his soul. He'd been making fun of her, pure and simple.

Unbidden came the memory of her mother's recuperation from major surgery several years ago. The normally stoic Gail Stuart had behaved in sometimes frightening, emotional ways. Mrs. Stuart later described her state as one of disconnectedness, in which she seemed to have no control over her brain or her emotions. A condition she'd blamed on the aftereffects of the anesthetic.

Nicholas had undergone surgery for his separated shoulder. According to Dyan, he'd been under the anesthetic for almost two hours while they inserted a pin.

Rachel mentally slapped herself. Nicholas was right about one thing. She suffered from a chronic case of niceness. Assigning genuine emotion to a man like him. He played the field because he was immature. He wasn't incapable of falling in love. He was incapable of settling down. A kid in a candy store, he couldn't settle on one piece of candy.

And if he could, he sure wouldn't pick Rachel Stuart.

Rachel sank down in the chair Nicholas had abandoned. Where had that ridiculous thought come from? She didn't care if Nicholas could fall in love. She cared about clearing her father. She didn't want Nicholas's heart. She wanted his detecting skills.

The sound of creaking wicker came from the porch. Rachel acknowledged another nagging thought. Nicholas had less trouble getting around. His ligaments and bones were healing. He'd soon abandon the crutch. And Rachel. Time was running out. She had to come up with some way to convince him to help her. And soon.

Shadows crept into the room, bringing the evening chill as the sun dipped below the western horizon. Rachel stirred, reluctant to leave the chair. Belatedly she realized the warmth she'd burrowed into came from

Nicholas. She sat where he'd been sitting. His body heat transferred to her body.

If only it were that easy to transfer her will to his brain.

There was no need the next morning to ask why Sharie Carter stood on the front doorstep before breakfast. The scent of warm, freshly baked cinnamon rolls perfumed the air.

Sharie held up the pan. "I wanted to do something to thank Nick for his help and comfort yesterday."

Rachel wanted to slam the door in Sharie's face. She stood back to let the other woman in.

Trailing behind her mother, Molly gave Rachel a brief smile and made a beeline for Nick. "I put in the raisins."

Rachel brought in coffee and dishes and pondered what Sharie had in mind. She was welcome to Nicholas. After he'd investigated for Rachel.

Nicholas was already feeding his face. "There's nothing a man appreciates like good home cooking," he said with gusto.

Rachel wondered what he thought she'd been feeding him. Ground glass sounded good right about now.

"I have to confess, I'm buttering you up a little," Sharie said.

Nicholas paused, the roll halfway to his mouth. "Oh?"

"It's my sister in Denver. She's dating this man. She thinks he's wonderful, but there's something about him. I thought maybe you could check him out."

Rachel hadn't expected such cleverness from Sharie.

Nicholas put down his cinnamon roll. "That's not the kind of investigative work we do."

"I'd pay, of course. One thing about Tom, he was

generous with the divorce settlement. He didn't want a fuss.''

"I can give you the name of a private detective in Denver. Charging you for our agency's specialized expertise when you don't need it would be highway robbery.''

"You helped Ian find his dog. I thought...'' Sharie bit her lip, her eyes beading with moisture. "I don't want your whole agency. I want you. To help me, I mean.''

Rachel thought everyone in the room knew what Sharie wanted.

Nicholas crumbled his roll on his plate. "Dollface,'' he eventually said absently, "pour me some more coffee, will you?''

"Dollface?'' Sharie asked.

He laughed self-consciously. "Sorry, it's a joke. Ian persists in believing I'm some kind of cross between a superspy and a private eye on TV. When he seemed to expect a special name for my 'you know,' as he calls Rachel, I came up with Dollface.''

"Rachel and you? I thought... Mrs. McDonnel said something about her being your nurse.''

"Nurse?'' Nicholas hooted. "Rachel can't stand the sight of blood.''

Only the knowledge she'd have to clean it up kept Rachel from flinging the pot of coffee at him. How dare he insinuate he and she slept together? He could darned well figure out some other way to discourage Sharie.

Rachel opened her mouth to set Sharie straight, then promptly swallowed her words. One didn't look a gift horse in the mouth. Nicholas wanted to use her? Fine. He could use her. Happily. With her blessing.

If he thought the self-satisfied smirk riding his face made him look like a man who was slightly embarrassed at broadcasting his private life, he was dead wrong. Rachel wondered how self-satisfied a smirk he'd be able to muster when she presented him with the bill for hiding behind one Rachel Stuart. He'd find the cost came high. Very high.

Satisfaction and triumph bubbled within her. She'd stumbled onto the key to obtaining Nicholas's aid. No, not stumbled. Nicholas had handed her the key in a gift-wrapped package. He claimed he couldn't be bribed or blackmailed or threatened. Rachel wanted to laugh out loud.

Nicholas Bonelli could be blackmailed all right. One simply had to know his weak spot. And now Rachel knew it. The one thing he feared. A woman getting her hooks into him. Sharie Carter wasn't the only threat on Nicholas's horizon.

Rachel had been incredibly dense and blind not to see it before. Nicholas's mother had practically drawn Rachel a picture, and she'd still missed it. One woman stood between Nicholas Bonelli and a horde of women with one thought in mind. Becoming Mrs. Nicholas Bonelli. Nicholas could claim the women he escorted knew the rules of the game. Knowing them was one thing. Rachel suspected each and every woman Nicholas dated, secretly believed she was the one woman who could capture Nicholas's heart.

Those women would leap at any opportunity to finagle their way deeper into Nicholas's life. Injured, needing assistance, Nicholas was highly vulnerable. Rachel Stuart provided his sole protection. The one person between Nicholas Bonelli and a trip down the matrimony aisle.

If Nicholas really wanted Rachel to leave, he'd have figured out a way to drive her away. But Nicholas didn't want her to leave. He hated needing help. He hated being vulnerable. But he wasn't stupid. He needed Rachel. The one woman who wouldn't barter her assistance for a wedding ring.

All Rachel had to do was threaten to step out of the picture, leaving him defenseless. His family had made their position clear. Nicholas would be stuck calling one of his lady friends for help. And once one of those ladies moved in with him, it would take dynamite to move her out.

The sense of time running out temporized her giddiness. Nicholas improved in strength and health every day. She had to press her advantage while he needed her services.

Sharie continued to gush about how she didn't know about Nicholas and Rachel. Obviously embarrassed, every word from her runaway tongue further illustrated her plans for Nicholas had included more than hiring him.

It was time to raise the stakes. Rachel walked around the table and poured Nicholas more coffee before casually leaning against his good shoulder. "I'd appreciate you not spreading this around, Sharie. Sometimes Nicky's sense of humor gets out of hand. Like calling me Dollface." She lovingly tousled his hair. "There's nothing wrong with our living together—" Nicholas twitched at her side "—but I'm a schoolteacher. Parents hold teachers to unrealistic standards. Nicky and I don't want to be rushed into marriage because a few parents think a teacher who isn't celibate will lead their children astray."

Nicholas dropped his cinnamon roll.

"I won't tell a soul," Sharie promised. "I know how it is. You wouldn't believe the things people think about a young, attractive secretary." She proceeded to enlighten them.

With victory soon to be Rachel's, listening to Sharie's indignant horror stories was a small price to pay. As was the fiercely hot arm which bound her hips to Nicholas's side. His idea of punishment for her putting into words and action his subtleties about their relationship. Hunger accounted for the strange feelings deep in her stomach. Hunger pangs brought on by eating nothing but cinnamon rolls for breakfast.

Sharie broke off her monologue on office intrigues. "Where's Molly?"

Three pairs of eyes spotted the open French doors at the same time. Rachel and Sharie raced for the sunporch and out the door to the deck, Nicholas clumping along in their wake. Rachel breathed a sigh of relief as she spotted Molly down on the wooden dock. Standing perilously close to the edge, the child leaned over to study something in the water below her. Rachel trotted down the sloping path to the dock.

Sharie let out an electrifying shriek. "Molly, be careful!"

The startled child lost her balance and fell off the dock.

"She can't swim!" Sharie screamed. "Save her, save her. Nick, save her! I can't swim. She'll drown! She'll drown!"

Rachel flew across the dock and leaped into the lake.

Cold, dark water closed over her head. She battled her way to the surface. Pollen floating on the water clogged her eyelashes. She couldn't see Molly. She managed one gulp of air before the water dragged her down again. Fighting her panic, her innate sense of survival, Rachel forced herself not to beat at the water. She had to stay down here, to search for Molly.

Opening her eyes under water had to be the most difficult thing she'd ever done. Her heart almost exploded in fear when a small fish swam past her face. Molly was nowhere in sight. Rachel's lungs screamed for air.

She battled her way to the lake's surface and managed to collect one quick breath before sinking again. Nicholas had lied to her the first day. The water rose above her head. She couldn't walk to shore. Her feet touched the bottom. Slippery stones. Acres of slippery stones, but no Molly. Rachel groped among the rocks. Molly had to be here somewhere. Molly. Rachel repeated the little girl's name over and over again, a mantra to keep her terror at bay. Find Molly. Then she could panic.

The pain in her lungs told her she needed air. No. Molly first. But the instinct for survival could not be denied. Without meaning or wanting to, Rachel flailed upward.

Choking and gasping, she breathed in precious air in the few seconds her head rose above the water. As she sank, a large object hit the water beside her with a resounding splash. Her arm bumped a solid object, and instinctively Rachel grabbed it. Her head popped above the water's surface again.

"Damn it, Rachel, hang on!"

Rachel blinked the water from her eyes. She clutched a round life preserver. Tiny steamers of white paint floated on the water's surface in the wake of the ring. Nicholas needed to repaint it. The preserver moved through the water, tugging at Rachel's arm. Trying to escape her. Nicholas would kill her if she let go. She tightened her grip.

A rock banged her knee. Rachel cried out, and the strain on her arms ceased. She sunk to her hands and knees, the pointed rocks digging into her. Rachel heard splashing, and pale lavender slacks moved into her field of vision.

"Can you stand up?" Sharie grabbed Rachel under her arms.

"Hell, yes, she can stand up. She doesn't need you playing lifeguard. Rachel, get out of that water."

Rachel struggled to her feet. Brushing off Sharie's ineffectual help, she labored toward shore.

Nicholas reached out with his good hand and yanked her up the rocky slope. "You are a blooming idiot," he raged. "The stupidest woman it has ever been my misfortune to meet."

"Molly?" Rachel managed to gasp.

"Molly swam to shore," Nicholas said in a cold, hard voice.

"Isn't she clever?" Sharie wrung out her pant legs.

"Hand me the other blanket you brought out from the house," Nicholas snapped at Sharie. "She's shivering like a leaf. What the hell were you thinking?" he snarled at Rachel. "Never mind. You couldn't be bothered to stop and think."

"Molly can't swim," Rachel hiccuped, burrowing into the blessedly warm, dry blanket Nicholas threw over her shoulders.

"Yes, I can," Molly piped up. "Ian taught me. I swim like Scotty. We dog-paddle." A bedraggled, blanket-wrapped Molly grinned up at Rachel.

"That's wonderful, Molly." Chattering teeth punctuated Rachel's words.

"Sure it's wonderful. She saved herself," Nicholas said savagely, "while a stupid, lamebrain, idiotic, half-witted, damned nincompoop tried to commit suicide."

"Why are you using bad words and yelling at Rachel?" Molly asked.

"Because she can't swim." He yanked the dripping life preserver from the lake and threw it violently to the ground.

Molly's mouth quivered. "I don't like it when you yell."

Nicholas took a deep breath, but before he could say anything, Sharie asked incredulously, "You can't swim?" She threw her arms around a shivering Rachel and hugged her tightly. "You did the bravest thing I've ever heard of."

"There was nothing brave about it. It was rash, heedless, stupid, and just plain dumb. What the hell was she going to do if Molly hadn't saved herself? She'd be more likely to pull her under and drown her than rescue her."

"Stop harassing her."

"Sharie, it's okay," Rachel said wearily.

"No, it's not okay. Maybe Molly did save herself, and maybe he did have to rescue you, but that's no reason for him to yell and swear at you. Pack your things and come home with us. I'm not leaving you with this inhuman monster."

"I can't—"

"She's not going anywhere except to the shower. What the hell are you doing standing around out here in the wind? I've got better things to do than take care of you if you get sick. Go inside and take a shower. Now." He saw her mouth open. "I don't want to hear one more word from you. Do it before I throw you back in the damned lake."

Without a word Rachel turned and slogged around the dock and up the path to the deck. Behind her a storm of angry voices broke out.

Molly's shrill tones carried into the house with Rachel. "You're mean and I don't like you anymore, Nick."

Hot water streaming over her finally stung Rachel's numbed, chilled body back to life. She slumped under the showerhead, abandoning herself to the sybaritic pleasures of cascading warmth, and occupied her mind by devising witty and cutting replies she might have said to shut Nicholas up and shame him for his unfair, beastly remarks.

Rinsing the soap from her hair, she applied conditioner. He had no right to call her names. So what if she couldn't swim? Sharie wasn't going after Molly and a fat lot of good Nicholas would have been with a still-healing, surgically repaired shoulder and casts on his arm and leg. If he'd jumped in, she would have had to rescue him, too.

So she'd jumped without waiting to see if Molly could swim. And maybe she'd jumped without checking if there was another way to save Molly. Okay, yes, she'd jumped without thinking.

That didn't justify Nicholas throwing a childish temper tantrum. The man totally lost control. You scared him half to death. The voice seemed to descend from the showerhead. Rachel knew it came from her own inner conscience.

She faced the truth. Nicholas Bonelli was right and she was wrong. Her rash behavior had not only endangered herself, she'd endangered others. Sharie couldn't swim, which meant, if Rachel hadn't been able to hang on to the life preserver, or if Nicholas hadn't had one handy or had such good aim, he would have felt compelled to come in the water after her. Handicapped as he was, and Rachel had to admit it, the way she had a slight tendency, okay, a huge tendency, to come unglued in water, she'd probably have drowned them both.

All because she'd acted first, and thought later. Way later. Picking up the wide-toothed comb, she combed the conditioner through her hair, loosening the snarls and tangles in the long, loose curls.

The comb caught on a knot in her hair. The resultant pain didn't sting nearly as much as the thought which hit her out of the blue. Darn and double darn. Just when she'd figured out how to force Nicholas to do her bidding, he had to go and rescue her. The man fouled up everything. As determined as she was to clear her father, she couldn't blackmail her rescuer.

Unless his nasty behavior canceled any obligation. If he'd been gracious about rescuing her, the situation would be different. As it was, any man who threw a

temper tantrum because a woman didn't drown didn't
deserve mercy. In fact, she'd tell him straight-out. If he
hadn't behaved so abominably, she would have changed
her mind about forcing him to help her. That would
teach him to think before he opened his mouth and hollered at her. Think of the consequences, she always told
her students. Nicholas should have considered the consequences of his temper tantrum.

You mean the way you considered the consequences
before you leaped off the dock? her inner voice jeered.
A conscience was a tedious, loathsome handicap.
Wrenching off the water, she reached around the shower
curtain, fumbled for the bath towel, wrapped it snugly
around her body, and stepped from the shower.

"About time. I thought I was going to have to toss a
life preserver in there."

"What are you doing in here?" Rachel gripped her
towel and peered across the steam-filled room at the man
sitting on the closed bathroom commode. "How'd you
get upstairs?"

"Slowly. What were you doing in there? Teaching
yourself how to swim? You took so long, I'd have
thought you'd drowned if I hadn't seen you moving."

"Seen me?" Rachel repeated indignantly. She tightened the slipping towel around her. "You mean you've
been sitting out here watching me through the shower
curtain?"

"I couldn't actually see you," he said curtly. "Your
elbows kept poking out the shower curtain."

His words failed to appease her. "You didn't answer
my question. What are you doing in here?"

"Making sure you're okay. What'd you think? That
since we're living together, I planned to join you in the
shower?"

She immediately reacted to the emphasis he'd put on
the words "living together." "Don't blame that on me.

You're the one who told Sharie I was your 'you know.' Before you opened your mouth you knew how she'd interpret those words. Exactly the way you meant her to.''

Nicholas didn't deny it. ''I expected you to leap in and call me a liar.'' He rubbed his shoulder. ''In fact, the more I think about it, the more I wonder why you didn't.'' He hauled his body off the commode and limped over to Rachel. ''As provocative as that skimpy towel is, and as good as you smell—'' he slid a finger along her collarbone ''—and as soft as you feel, you can't use a mythical affair to sway me into doing what you want.''

The cloud of steam in the bathroom fogged her mind. All she could think about was how she preferred brown eyes to any other color. A preference she'd never noticed before. His finger singed her skin. She had trouble breathing. He couldn't help but notice. ''From the lake,'' she said aloud. ''My lungs haven't recovered.''

''Nothing about me has recovered. When you leaped off the dock...'' His fingers tightened convulsively on her shoulder. ''I promised myself after I hauled you out, I'd throw you right back in again, I was so damned mad at you.'' He trailed his fingers to the base of her neck where he gently pressed his thumb against the pulse beating in her throat.

Her pulse drummed riotously in her ears. ''I'm sorry, I didn't mean...'' Impossible to speak, to think, with his gaze riveted on her mouth. A rivulet of water ran down her leg. She clutched her towel to her chest, wishing the terry cloth muffled the sound of her shallow breathing.

''You're sorry,'' he softly repeated her words. Nicholas moved his hand from her throat to her back. ''Sorry enough you wouldn't do it again?''

''Yes.'' The word came out almost a sigh. She ought to push him away, kick him out of the bathroom. She ought to dry off. Not that she needed to. Most of the water had evaporated from her overheated body.

Nicholas ran his fingers through her hair. "I wondered how you made it curl like that."

"It's natural." A few drops of water rained from her hair to the back of her legs.

"Like you're a natural liar?" A slow smile removed the sting from the insult.

"I'm not a liar." She couldn't remember what they were talking about. How could she with his hand on her back easing beneath the towel? The heat from his palm penetrated every layer of her body until her innermost core threatened to burst into flame.

"Yes, you are." He gave a low, intimate laugh. "You know you would." He pressed her closer to him.

Would what? Kiss him? "Yes, I would."

"Damned with your own mouth." He lowered his head.

"Yes." She closed her eyes. And suddenly she was drowning again. Warm, insistent currents caught her up, tossing her with abandon into uncharted waters. Almost in panic she clutched Nicholas around his waist. His sweatshirt shifted in her grasp, inviting exploration. As he explored her mouth. Her fingers slid beneath his shirt to glide over warm, silken skin. She loved the taste of him, the smell of him, the feel of him. His demanding, possessive mouth, his solid, muscled back, his hard chest. The tiny, sharp gasp of pain—

Rachel jumped backward. "I'm sorry. Did I hurt you? I don't know what I was thinking. I didn't mean to press against your arm like that. Are you okay?"

"You are the damnedest woman, Rachel Stuart." A wry smile touched the corners of his mouth.

"I'm sorry. I don't know… It must have been all the excitement."

"There's going to be even more excitement if you don't pull up that towel," Nicholas said dryly.

Rachel pulled it up. If it was red, it would match the color of her face. "What are you doing in here, anyway?"

"I told you. I wanted to make sure you're okay."

"I'm fine."

"Better than fine, judging by that kiss." Lazy male satisfaction filled his voice.

Rachel eyed him squarely on the tip of his nose. "You can wipe that arrogant 'what a big boy am I' tone out of your voice. That kiss was merely an exuberant celebration of life. It's natural when one has cheated death."

He made a disgusted sound. "The closest you came to death out there was when you reached the shore. I'd have murdered you then, but I thought Molly might object."

"You're the one who told me the water wasn't that deep."

"Elsewhere along the shore it isn't. You decided to play heroine in the middle of the channel dredged out from the boathouse."

"I think we've exhausted the subject of my little swim, so please leave so I can get dressed."

Nicholas stepped backward to rest his hip on the bathroom vanity. "We haven't begun to exhaust the subject."

"I made a mistake, okay? I acted in a rash, unthinking manner. I'm sorry. I won't do it again. What do you want from me? I'm not going to get down on my hands and knees."

"Yes, you will."

"I will not. You are—" The hand over her mouth cut off her indignant words.

"Not the hands and knees bit. You'd jump in the lake again." He grinned at her sputtering. "You can't help yourself. You're like a fire horse responding to the fire siren. One cry for help and you leap into action. Or into the lake.''

She tried to shake her head, but he tightened his grip. Her lips, sensitized by his kisses, throbbed against his warm palm. She ought to bite his hand. She commanded him to let go.

He laughed at her gobbled words. ''If I didn't know better, Teach, I'd say you were using bad words.'' The glare she gave him failed to squelch his amusement. ''Be careful. Molly doesn't like bad words.'' The merriment faded from his eyes. ''If anyone should get down on his hands and knees, it's me.'' He gave her a crooked smile. ''But if I did get down, you'd have to help me up, and I'm not all that sure you'd bother. I'm the one who owes the apology.'' His eyes darkened. ''I've never felt so helpless. Sharie screaming 'Molly can't swim,' and a turtle could have beat me down to the lake. Then you jumped in and you can't swim—'' He stopped, his jaw clenching.

Only then did Rachel remember Nicholas had only one good arm. He wasn't holding her to him. She could step away from the hand over her mouth anytime she wanted. Her legs wouldn't move.

''Sharie kept yelling at me to hurry up, to do something, and I was fumbling with one hand to untie that old life preserver my mom tied on the deck for decoration. I didn't even know if the damned thing could float.'' Removing his hand from her mouth, he tapped his knuckles on the vanity top. ''Every time I looked, your head was going under again.''

''I'm fine.'' She couldn't think of anything else to say.

''I knew how scared you must be.'' He didn't look at her, but watched his knuckles thudding against the ceramic tile. ''It was too horrible to think of you drowning when you're so frightened of water.''

Rachel touched his arm. "It's over. Everyone's okay."

He grabbed her fingers, squeezing them. "I was so relieved when you grabbed the preserver and hung on, I guess I sort of snapped. I wanted to hug you and make sure you were okay and all I could do was yell and swear at you. Like Sharie said, I'm some kind of monster."

"You are not a monster of any kind. But you are squeezing the blood out of my fingers. Thank you." Rachel wiggled her fingers. They smarted as the blood surged back through them. With the pain came the knowledge she'd just kissed goodbye any plan for forcing Nicholas into doing her bidding. She couldn't, not after his heartfelt confession. She mustered up a resigned smile. "Do you think I didn't know why you were yelling? I'm a teacher. Kids fall off the swing set, and frighten me so badly, I want to shake them until their teeth rattle."

"But you don't," he said heavily.

"I don't shake them. But once I've bandaged them up, and hugged them, I give them a lecture on playground safety which practically curls their hair."

He wrapped a strand of her damp hair around his finger. "Sharie was right. You were magnificently brave."

Rachel's eyes flew to his face to see if he was teasing her. His steady, dead-serious gaze roused her conscience. Nicholas deserved the truth. "I wasn't brave. At first I didn't even think. Then I was terrified. I almost panicked, like my first day here when I fell off the dock."

"Listen, Dollface." He spoke in a gravelly voice. "The first thing a babe like you's gotta learn is no arguing with the gumshoe. I'm the boss, see?"

Rachel pursed her lips. "Why do you get to be boss? I want to be boss. You can be the bimbo secretary."

He shook his head and limped to the door and opened it. "Neither of us is going to be the bimbo secretary," he said over his shoulder. "I'm the hotshot detective and you're Dollface." Turning he swept her towel-draped body with an extravagant leer, then winked at her. "My client with the great legs." He shut the bathroom door with the tip of his crutch.

CHAPTER SEVEN

NICHOLAS liked her legs. At his astonishing words, her chin had dropped practically to the top of those so-called great legs. He'd called her his client with—

Rachel dashed out the bathroom door. "Nicholas, wait a minute."

Halfway down the staircase, he balanced on the crutch and turned slowly around. "What happened to Nicky?"

"Nicky?" She skidded to a stop at the top of the steps.

"I guess you're right," he said with mock solemnity. "A client calling me Nicky doesn't sound so good."

"Are you serious? Do you mean it?"

"Yes. You'd better start calling me Mr. Bonelli."

"Not that." She moved down the steps until she stood with her face level with his. "You said 'client.' Are you really going to investigate for me?"

"I wasn't speaking gibberish under the influence of painkillers, if that's what you're worried about." He scowled at her. "But the damned medication must have weakened my brain." He turned and continued his painstaking journey down the stairs.

Rachel ran after him, her bare feet padding down the wooden steps. "Why are you agreeing to clear my father?"

"I'm not agreeing to clear your father. I'm agreeing to investigate the circumstances of the crime." Safe at the bottom of the stairs, Nicholas swung around on his crutch and looked disapprovingly at her. "There's no point wasting my time investigating if you're not going to accept what I find. I don't go into an investigation

looking for evidence which supports my, or your, or anyone else's cockeyed theory. I go into it with an open
mind, and if you can't do the same, we'll forget the
whole business right now.''

"I'll keep an open mind.''

"People don't always like what I dig up," he warned.

"I'll like it. My dad's innocent." At the darkening
look on his face, she added hastily, "I promise, I'll accept whatever you find out.''

"One other thing. You need to understand how our
little arrangement is going to work. It's my show. I don't
want any suggestions from you. I don't want any arguments over what I'm doing, and I don't want you nagging me.''

Rachel didn't bother to agree to the ridiculous con-
ditions. His change of heart interested her far more.
"Why are you agreeing to investigate, when you absolutely refused me before?''

"I hadn't seen your legs before.''

Her stomach dipped. Not at his teasing words, but at
the unpleasant suspicion aroused by them. "Your agree-
ment doesn't have anything to do with what just happened, does it?''

He gave her an impatient look. "It has everything to
do with it.''

She blinked at the unvarnished truth. She'd been
wrong in believing sex meant more to him than a bar-
gaining chip. Disappointment and sadness settled over
her. And thankfulness. She'd been in danger of liking
him. This proved his shallowness and lack of honor. And
his multiple charms. To her horror, in spite of everything, the prospect of sleeping with Nicholas appealed.
She suspected he would be a fantastic lover. But not her
lover. Her fingers clutched spasmodically at her towel.
"I won't sleep with you. Not even to clear my father.''

Nicholas's jaw went slack with disbelief, then turned

to granite. "I realize this is the age of women's liberation," he said sarcastically, "but before you reject it, you might wait for an invitation to climb into my bed."

Rachel refused to back down. "You said the only reason you're going to investigate is because of our kiss just now."

His eyes suddenly danced with laughter. "Dollface, your mind travels down the most unexpected paths. You never say or do what I expect." A sudden flame flared in brown depths. "I have a feeling sleeping with you would be like parachute-jumping. Hurling oneself into space, beautiful, exhilarating free fall, and then drifting slowly back to earth, safe and satisfied."

The sensuous words delivered in a low, almost caressing voice caused Rachel's pulse to riot and totally destroyed her brain cells. She stared mutely at Nicholas.

A tiny smile played at the corner of his lips. "I'll have to remember this. There are two ways to shut you up."

She turned fiery red, knowing instantly the second way he had in mind was kissing her.

"I won't say I don't want to sleep with you," Nicholas said. "I admit to a certain curiosity as to what sex with you would be like, but you're the kind of woman who couldn't separate sex from love." He ran a finger down her bare arm. "You deserve a man who can give you both. I can't."

"Yes, you can." The sound of her own husky voice startled Rachel from her trancelike state. Before Nicholas could respond to her inane statement, she amplified it. "Give some woman love, I mean. I don't believe you are incapable of loving a woman. Never mind," she added hastily as he made to speak. "That's neither here nor there. If you weren't referring to, well—" she blushed hotly "—investigating because you wanted to sleep with me, what did you mean?"

"You shouldn't use white towels. There's too much contrast between them and your bright red skin."

"Very funny." She jerked away from the finger stroking her arm. "Are you going to explain your change of mind or not?"

"What if I said not? What would you do then?"

She studied his face. The crooked smile didn't match the serious eyes. "I guess I'd think," she said slowly, "you're an honorable man who feels a moral obligation to seek the truth."

Her words wiped all expression from his face. Then he raised his brow the barest millimeter, mocking her. "Sincerity's my stock-in-trade."

"You're a big fake. You changed your mind because I raised a doubt in your mind whether or not justice was rendered."

He shook his head. "Justice has nothing to do with it. Your dad died. My dad has had to live with the knowledge he accidentally killed a man. That's not justice, that's a tragedy."

"Yes." Rachel blinked away the scratchiness in her eyes. "All right. Forget justice. You care about finding out the truth."

"Rachel, I know the truth. I'm agreeing to your investigation for one reason, and one reason only. Today you demonstrated that beneath the freckles and the ridiculous jewelry is an inner core of steel. You, Teach, are one hell of a tough little nut. Some people would say you deserve the truth. I don't give a damn about deserving. What I think is you're tough enough to accept the truth." His voice hardened. "I'm betting on it, Dollface. Don't let me down."

Rachel paced back and forth on the deck, fingering the large dinosaur hanging from her neck.

"Would you stop pacing? You're making me dizzy.

Or maybe what you're wearing is making me dizzy. Is there supposed to be some significance to blue and white stripes and a reptile?''

She glanced down at her blouse and slacks. ''They're periwinkle, and this is a brachiosaurus. Some of them lived in what is now Colorado. They were eighty-two-feet long and weighed as much as fifty tons.''

''And you wish you had a pet one to sic on my father.''

''He'd be safe. Brachiosauruses were herbivores, not carnivores.''

''You know the most useless information.''

''When you're teaching first grade, knowing about dinosaurs isn't merely useful, it's mandatory.'' Rachel froze at the sound of a car door slamming. Voices, old and young, male and female, carried down to the deck.

From the time Nicholas's filthy rich railroad ancestor built the lakeside vacation home, family members traditionally spent July Fourth there. Nicholas had suggested Rachel invite her mother and brother to join the festivities, but she'd declined. She had to spend two days in the company of her father's killer, but her family didn't need to be subjected to the same ordeal.

Not that it seemed an ordeal on the surface. From the moment of their arrival, Nicholas's mother, sister and niece, fluttered around Nicholas, hugging and kissing him, patting his good shoulder, inquiring solicitously about his injuries, and outrageously spoiling him. He had only to think aloud he might want something and the desired object instantly appeared before him. Dyan's husband, Charlie, had cautiously slapped Nicholas on the back, then muttered darkly about malingerers and partners not pulling their loads, only to precipitously retreat when Nicholas threatened to return to work the next day.

''A lot we'd get done with every woman in the place shoving the others out of the way so she can be the one at your beck and call," Charlie grunted. "Until they found what a petty tyrant you are when you're out of commission. I feel sorry for poor Rachel, stuck up here with you bossing her around."

Nicholas hooted. "Poor Nick is more like it. This harmless-looking woman would give Nurse What's-her-name in that movie a run for her money when it comes to cruel and abusive. She actually forced me on an endurance hike."

"A couple hundred feet on a trail for the handicapped in Rocky Mountain National Park. There were lots of benches to sit on, and you enjoyed seeing the elk in the meadow."

"She threw my fish back." Nicholas looked mournfully at his dad and Charlie for commiseration.

"I wasn't going to cut their heads off, and you couldn't." Rachel tried to act naturally, but she knew Nicholas's father was studying her.

"I might as well have thrown the worms in the lake."

"Like I say at school, keep the monsters too busy to think about getting into trouble," Dyan said briskly.

"Are you calling your brother a monster?" Nicholas asked.

Dyan raised an inquisitive brow at Rachel. "Well? Is he?"

Rachel refused to take sides. Nicholas didn't seem to object to her arguing with him, but she doubted he'd appreciate her lining up with his sister. Having persuaded him to investigate, Rachel had no intention of giving him an excuse to change his mind. Not with his father here.

Apprehension knotted her stomach. For years she'd dreamed of, planned, and plotted this encounter. Now the moment was at hand, doubt and panic assailed her. If Nicholas's dad simply refused to answer any questions, or if he lied to her... No, she wouldn't consider that. She had enough experience as a teacher to spot a liar at a thousand yards. If Lt. Bonelli's answers were unacceptable, they'd have to dig deeper.

They. The enormous flaw in her plan exposed itself. All of the threats she'd so carefully compiled as a means of compelling Nicholas to do her bidding turned out to be useless. She had to rely on Nicholas's sense of honesty and fair play. He'd solved Ian's and Molly's problems.

But solving them cost him nothing. If he had to make a choice between Rachel and his father... She knew the answer to that one. It was no choice. Just as choosing between her father and Nicholas would never be a real choice. Fathers came first. Didn't they?

After lunch, Charlie and Dyan readied the small sailboat from the boathouse. If one could call eighteen feet small, Rachel thought, watching as they snapped masts upright and hauled out sails. The children scrambled over the boat as surefooted and knowledgeable as the adults. Mrs. Bonelli settled herself serenely in the boat and waved to her husband who stood on the dock, seeing them off.

Rachel tensed as he turned and headed up to the house.

"He's harmless," Nicholas said.

Rachel didn't bother to refute the ridiculous statement. Nicholas's father might be a lot of things, including a high-ranking muckety-muck in the Colorado Springs Police Department, but she very much doubted he was harmless.

He looked like Nicholas. A little older, a little shorter, not as trim, and more than a few strands of gray had cropped up in the wavy, blue-black hair, but his eyes, encased in a network of deep lines, were carbon copies of Nicholas's dark brown eyes. When he'd laughed at Nicholas's tale of investigating Scotty's disappearance, the same deep amusement warmed his eyes. When he scowled at a careless boater on the lake, his irises darkened to the same bitter chocolate color.

He'd turned those dark eyes on Rachel more than a few times since he'd arrived. Studying her. Judging her. Wondering what he could get away with telling her? Or wondering how it felt to be the daughter of a criminal? Except she wasn't. Her dad was innocent. Which no one knew better than the man walking slowly, almost reluctantly, up to the deck.

Maybe he hated to see women cry, too. Dyan's children, Andy and JoJo, visibly adored him. Which meant nothing. She'd read that gangsters' grandchildren frequently adored them.

Nicholas and she had argued about telling him in advance they wanted to talk to him about Rachel's father. That wasn't quite true. Rachel had argued against telling. Nicholas had reminded her he was not only the one with investigative experience, he knew his father. Then he'd simply ignored her arguments, her requests and her reasoning.

Lunch refused to settle in her stomach. For the first time she questioned what she'd begun. Pushing a rock downhill was easy. The difficult part was controlling where the rock went. Her father was dead, with few people knowing the sordid circumstances surrounding his death. Maybe she should be content with that. No. She couldn't be. He was innocent.

Pulling up a weathered deck chair, Lt. Bonelli took a pipe out of a jacket pocket. "Eva, Nick's mom, made me give up smoking years ago, but I still chew on the filthy thing."

A swallow swooped low over the water. As he lifted into the air, Rachel let out the breath she'd been holding.

Lt. Bonelli sat back in his chair and pulled down the brim of his hat to shade his eyes from the fierce July sun. "You probably don't remember, but I saw you that day."

She would have sworn she remembered every detail of that horrible day. She didn't remember Nicholas's father being there.

"I sat in an unmarked police car while the lieutenant went in to tell your mother. You were all skinny arms and legs with a mop of bright red hair glinting in the sun. It was unseasonably warm that September, and the car windows were down. Your brother came over to the car to ask who I was. You marched after him to give him a sermon on talking to strangers."

"She must have been born bossy," Nicholas said.

A motorboat roared past. Too close to shore, it sent waves dashing against the rocks. The dock rocked, making Rachel glad they sat up on the deck. Just watching the rocking dock made her nauseous.

"You gave me the most suspicious look." Joseph Bonelli smiled slightly. "Your eyes were too big for your face. Later I tried to tell Eva their color, but I failed miserably."

"A green beer bottle, with the sun shining through the glass," Nicholas said.

Joseph Bonelli squinted at her. "I believe you're right. Anyway—" he sucked on the pipe stem "—the lieutenant came out then and your mother called you both into the house."

His words brought it back. Her mother had been so quiet, so calm. Their father was dead, she said. Killed by a policeman in his car. They said her father had stolen money, but that wasn't true. He wasn't a thief. No matter what anyone said, he wasn't a thief. He loved them. He wouldn't have left them. He wasn't a thief. Rachel's mother had repeated those three sentences over and over again. That day, that week, until they became cemented in their brains. The words formed the rock wall which held them up, supported them through the hard times, the bad times.

At night her mother had sobbed alone in the dark. Sometimes in her room, sometimes roaming through the house. Rachel never spoke of hearing her, not even to Tony. She wondered if he'd lain awake at night hearing the pain and anguish, as helpless as Rachel to make it better. Wondered if he'd soaked his pillow with tears, as she'd soaked hers.

One other thing their mother had drummed into them. They were never, ever to tell anyone, not even their very best friends, what the policemen said their father had done. Because the police were wrong.

And now Rachel sat on the deck, clutching the hand of the son of one of the policemen. She blinked. When had she grabbed Nicholas's hand?

Taking the pipe from his mouth, Joseph Bonelli tapped the bowl on the arm of the chair before sticking the stem back in his mouth. "Nicholas said you had questions about your father. What do you want to know?"

"I don't believe he sold the information in Parker and Thane's sealed bids to their competitors."

"She thinks you framed him," Nicholas said baldly. "You or Robert Thane."

Joseph Bonelli took his pipe out of his mouth and stared dumbfounded at his son. Nick shrugged.

As if to say she was delusional and an idiot. Rachel jerked free her hand. "It could have happened that way," she said. "My dad was not a thief."

Her words seemed to freeze the three of them in suspended animation. Rachel felt as if she were floating above her body, observing the scene from a distance. Out on the lake a loud snap sounded as a gust of wind suddenly filled the slack sail of a small passing boat. Voices and the smell of gasoline from a motorboat traveled across the water. Houses across the lake, which had been quiet and shuttered, had come alive for the holiday, with ant-size humans populating docks and roaming the lakeshores. The scent of barbecue grills filled the air.

"I see," Joseph Bonelli finally said. "I didn't quite understand what Nicholas had in mind." He sighed. "Suppose you tell me what you know."

Rachel told him.

"That's what your mother told you?"

"Are you calling her a liar?"

He didn't immediately answer, and when he did, he manifestly selected his words with care. "Your mother and you and your brother were the true victims of your father's crime. She was left alone to raise two children." He hesitated. "We all make mistakes and wrong choices, but most people have good intentions. The sad ones are those who know their choices are wrong, but they are too weak to resist temptation. They tell themselves it's not wrong, or they deserve whatever it is they want. Their excuses number in the thousands."

"My father wasn't weak."

He continued as if she hadn't spoken. "The captain assured your mother, with your father dead, Thane wanted the books closed on the affair. I'm not sure why your mother told you anything about it. There was no reason for you to know. No reason to taint your memories."

"I don't want any of your insulting platitudes," Rachel said tightly. "Nothing could taint my memories of my father." Nicholas put his hand on her arm. Telling her to calm down, be civil—she didn't know what. Or care. Beyond civilities, she flung his hand off. "Don't call him a criminal. He wasn't."

"He admitted it. Signed a confession. He'd put the money in a bank account." Joseph Bonelli looked around the deck. Everywhere but at Rachel. "Stuart said he wanted the money for his family. For a larger home, to start a college fund for his kids. He must have loved you very much.''

''Oh, no, that won't work,'' Rachel said shakily. ''You can't convince me he did it, so you're trying to make me think he did it for me, make me feel guilty so I'll quit asking questions.''

''My dear, I didn't mean—''

''Stow it, Rachel. There's no room for melodrama in an investigation.'' Nicholas turned to his father. ''Is the confession on file? She'll want to read it.''

''If she really wants to, I probably can arrange it. I'm not sure it's a good idea.''

''Don't worry about Rachel. The lady's got guts. When we get back to town, we'll come in and read the confession.''

Rachel shot out of her chair, furious at Nicholas's assumptions. ''That's it? He tells you there's a confession and you believe it? Maybe you already knew about it. Maybe the two of you contrived the whole story over the phone. Throw Rachel a morsel, like a confession, to shut her up. Then she'll go meekly away and not make any more waves. What makes you think I'd believe a confession handed to me by the man who—''

She'd forgotten how much faster Nicholas could move now that he'd abandoned the crutch and relied on his walking cast.

''Nod your head when you're through behaving irrationally, and I'll move my hand.''

Rachel nodded. The second Nicholas removed his hand from her mouth, she whirled to face his father. ''Arrest him. You're a cop. I want to charge him with assault and battery.''

''Forget it, Rachel,'' Nicholas said. ''I told you when we started this, you're supposed to keep your mouth shut and let me run the show. You came looking for me, so don't start flinging accusations around." He added flatly, "Addison and Bonelli don't manufacture evidence. We find what's there. Once we take on a client, we're always on the side of the client. No matter who's on the other side." He paused a moment as if to let his words sink in, then added, "If you don't like the way I'm handling this, you can call it quits anytime."

Rachel turned and ran into the house.

"She was going to say I'm the man who killed her father, wasn't she?" Joseph Bonelli's low-spoken words came clearly through the screened windows of the porch.

The French doors stood open to the porch. Rachel moved to the main room of the house and stepped to one side so she was hidden from the men's view. Resting her head against the peeled log walls, she waited for Nicholas's answer.

"Forget it, Dad," he said. "Rachel has red hair. You know what they say about redheads and temper."

"I don't want to tell you how to run your life, Nick, but I wish you hadn't gotten mixed up with her. I don't deny she's attractive, and I'm sure you feel some obligation since she's been helping you, but some things are better left alone. She really believes he didn't do it." He hesitated. "What happens when you prove he did?"

"Nothing happens," Nick said, "other than she knows the truth."

"I meant with you and her."

Rachel stopped breathing as she waited for Nicholas's answer.

"There is no me and her," he said.

Which is exactly how Rachel wanted it. There was no reason for the words to hurt so much.

Charlie grilled supper out on the dock. "In spite of all the unwanted advice and interference from Bonelli males, the hamburgers are perfect," he announced to his wife, setting down a platter of what appeared to be round charcoal briquettes.

His words set the tone for supper. Light, frivolous, teasing. No one noticed Rachel's lack of appetite. No one alluded to her father. Probably no one but Rachel noticed the way Joseph Bonelli avoided her. Except for Nicholas. Rachel observed him giving his father a puzzled frown more than once.

Dyan had other things on her mind. Other women, actually. Nicholas's women. "If you don't start listening to your messages, dear brother," she began her assault, "I'm going to publish your whereabouts in the newspaper."

"I pick up my messages."

"Try answering them," his sister retorted. "My phone has rung nonstop since you came up here."

"We need to have a little talk about how I 'came' up here."

"You can thank me later," Dyan said airily. "Now I want your women to leave me alone. Summer raves there's a great play on at the theater," Dyan spoke in a pretentious voice. "Allie wants to know if she should get tickets for the big musical coming to town. Tiffany's hot for handball." Dyan giggled at the comical leer her husband gave her. "Sydney bought some marvelous new feathers and she's tying magpie nymph flies or some such nonsense. Jessica whines about an artsy movie she wants you to see, and Bunnie wants you to—"

"Don't answer the phone," her unrepentant brother said. "Let the machine get it."

"I have children. They have friends. Other children who hate to leave messages."

"I talked to Yvonne," JoJo piped up. "She wants to take cowboy dance lessons. I didn't know cowboys danced."

"I talked to Jamie," her brother said, not to be outdone. "She wants to go to Central City to the opera. I wrote down her message," he added proudly.

"And Debbie said she'll take you sailing," Charlie said. "You won't have to lift a finger." He wiggled his eyebrows. "She mentioned warm sun, soothing water and a private cove."

Nicholas added more baked beans to his plate. "Tell them not to bother you. That I'll call when I'm released from the convalescent home."

Andy looked across the table. "I thought you were in Europe, Uncle Nick. Mama said so on the phone."

"It was just a little white lie, Andrew. Eat your potato salad." Dyan glared at Nicholas. "I had to say something. Couldn't you date women who aren't so determined and aggressive? Not only do they refuse to believe anything I say, they keep calling and calling. Bunnie, Summer and Tiffany actually came by my house. As if I were hiding you in the closet or something. I didn't think I'd ever get rid of them. You have to do something. If you don't—" she gave her brother a dark look "—I'll tell them you faked your injuries and you're really on your honeymoon."

Charlie hooted. "Who'd believe a confirmed bachelor like Nick on a honeymoon? Everybody knows he'll never get married."

"Perhaps if you went in for counseling, Nick," his mother said in a troubled voice. "It might help you find a woman."

Rachel couldn't help herself. The cumulative tensions of the afternoon found their release in an outbreak of semihysterical giggles. Everyone looked at her as if she'd lost her mind.

Then Nicholas laughed, and at the other end of the table, Charlie started guffawing. The children had no idea what the joke was, but joined in the laughter.

Eva Bonelli looked confused. "I enjoy a good laugh

as much as the next person, but I don't know what's so funny."

"The idea of Nick needing therapy to find a woman," Charlie gasped. "He needs castle walls and a moat to keep them away."

Eva gave her son-in-law a reproving look. "You wouldn't laugh at a blind man, and you shouldn't laugh at Nick's disability. You're a happily married man with a wife and two darling children. Poor Nick could have a million girlfriends and he'd still be alone."

Everyone around the table glanced at Nicholas and then quickly away. Rachel could scarcely believe it. Nicholas hadn't made up the stupid family tradition. They all believed he could never fall in love because he hadn't done it on some ridiculous timetable. As if one should fall in love on schedule. Rachel wanted to say Nicholas wasn't disabled. He was spoiled. No matter how true the words were, they probably weren't the most politic to say to Nicholas's mother. "My mouth has been watering ever since I saw that cake you brought, Mrs. Bonelli."

The blatant compliment distracted and soothed Nicholas's mother. "Call me Eva, dear. It's Nick's favorite dessert. Yellow cake with boiled icing and sliced bananas in the middle and lots of coconut sprinkled on top. Is everyone ready for it?"

Amid a chorus of approval, Rachel went after the cake.

They ate the dessert on the screened porch, then everyone bundled up in jackets and blankets and took their coffee or hot chocolate out on the deck for the fireworks display. Rachel would have escaped to her room if Nicholas hadn't caught her arm and brought her out on the deck.

Around the lake, lighted windows sent friendly beams into the dark night. Nearly a hundred boats with sails down and engines silenced floated on the lake, their running lights dancing around like fireflies. Cars jockeyed for parking along the few public areas of the lakeshore. Muted voices carried across the water. Andy and JoJo practically jumped out of their skins with anticipation and impatience.

"They shoot the fireworks off a barge in the lake," Nicholas said. He spoke his next words in her ear. "Now do you believe me? That I can't fall in love, I mean."

"I believe you believe it, but that doesn't make it true."

He reached over and tugged one of her curls. "Remember that, Teach. Believing something doesn't make it true."

He wasn't referring to some stupid family legend. He meant her father. Before Rachel could tell him what he could do with his warning, a rocket shot into the sky. A resounding boom reverberated off the mountains encircling the lake, and a spectacular cascade of red and green sparkles rained down on its reflection in the water. Andy and JoJo gave cries of wondrous appreciation while on the lake boaters honked in approval. Another rocket screamed upward to explode in a firefall of silver droplets. One after another, breathtakingly beautiful fireworks electrified the crowd.

The last year of his life, her father had taken them to Memorial Park to celebrate Independence Day. Rachel closed her eyes and let her mind drift back to that night. The spectacular fireworks. The outdoor concert put on by the symphony. In the background, her parents whispering angrily. Rachel's eyes popped open. Where had that come from? Her parents never fought. Why had she conjured up a false memory? The answer came on the heels of the question. Because of guilt. Consorting with the enemy. It was one thing to celebrate the Fourth of July with the Bonellis. Nicholas's hand rested warmly against the back of her neck. It was quite another to enjoy herself.

"That wasn't so bad, was it?"

Rachel waved until the car bearing JoJo and Andy back to Colorado Springs disappeared from view, then she turned slowly to give Nicholas the same look she'd give a giant cockroach. "If spending two days with a man who'd prefer you were invisible is your idea of a good time, it's not mine."

"You're accusing me of neglecting you? I didn't realize we had that kind of relationship."

"We don't have any kind of relationship at all," Rachel snapped. "Other than business," she quickly added. "I'm talking about your father. He could hardly wait for lunch to be over so he could leave."

"Sometimes Dad has trouble leaving work behind. His mind was probably on some case they're working."

Rachel held open the front door. "It wasn't that."

"You know him so well."

"I know when someone can hardly stand to be in the same room with me. He managed to hide his feelings until I told him point-blank my father wasn't a criminal."

Nick eased himself down onto the sofa. "Your imagination was working overtime."

"I suppose it was working overtime when it imagined your father lied about that mythical confession," she said bitterly.

"My father has never lied in his life."

His flat words sounded the death knoll to her plans. "I see," she said after a minute. Swallowing hard, she forced herself to continue. "You aren't going to help me, are you?"

CHAPTER EIGHT

"THAT depends on what you want help with," Nicholas said. "Proving your father is innocent or proving my father set him up or—"

"They're one and the same."

"Or," Nicholas repeated emphatically, "finding out the truth about what happened fifteen years ago."

"The truth is, my father was innocent."

"Then that's what we'll find out."

"Is it? When you're convinced he was a common criminal? You think he sold out the company he worked for. You think he stole money because his family wanted more than he could give. You think I'm the daughter of a thief. You think—"

"I think you're getting hysterical and I'll either have to kiss you or..."

The jesting remark killed all hope. Nicholas had no intention of helping her. "You've been humoring me. No—" The truth slowly dawned on her. "Worse than that. You did believe my threat about going to the newspapers. You and your father worked out a scheme to manufacture evidence of my father's guilt. You thought I was so stupid and gullible I'd believe it. I'd be thoroughly ashamed to be a criminal's daughter and I'd go away and never bother any of you again."

"Are you quite finished?" Nicholas asked coldly.

"I won't be finished until I prove my father didn't commit any crime."

"Am I supposed to applaud your stirring declaration?"

"Go ahead. Belittle me. I deserve your mockery. All

133

the time I was feeling sorry for you because I thought you were in pain, you were devising ways to deceive me. And I made it easy for you, didn't I?" Too angry to stand still, she stormed back and forth across the room. "I fell for the oldest trick in the book. Flattery." She stabbed the air with her fingers, punctuating her anger. "You were brilliant. You didn't bother flattering my hair or face or figure or cooking or mind. You went straight for my soft spot. The one thing I pride myself on. My strength. You mumbled a few inanities about me being a tough nut, and I was putty in your hands."

Nicholas rested his injured shoulder against the sofa back. "Let me know when you're through," he said in a bored voice. "I don't want to interrupt such a melodramatic performance."

She stopped in front of a window, staring sightlessly at the tall pine outside. There was no way to reach him, to make him care. Not about her. Rachel didn't want him to care about her. Her breath caught as the denial rang somehow false. No, she wouldn't deal with that now. Not now when he'd deceived her. Her arms fell limply to her sides. "I should have suspected your abrupt reversal of opinion. It came too sudden, too easily. The only thing you've changed since you came up here is your clothes." She had too much pride to cry in front of him. "I'll pack and leave this afternoon. How you get back to Colorado Springs is your problem. I'll call your mother tomorrow. Since I'm walking out on the job, she owes me nothing."

"Quitter."

Rachel fired up at the soft-spoken taunt, but the spark of outrage quickly flickered out. "You can't trick me into staying. Not now. Not when I know you're manipulating me." She wanted to scream, to throw things. Instead she headed for the stairs.

And promptly tripped over the step stool.

She landed on the sofa. In Nicholas's lap.

Wincing as she bounced against his arm, he maneuvered her to his side. "Damn. You must be taking lessons from that crook, Donet. If my clients are going to start acting like the guys I catch, I'm going to have to go into another line of business."

"Oh, Nicholas, I'm sorry. I wasn't watching where I was going. What can I do? Call a doctor? I can drive you to the nearest clinic. Did I hurt you badly?"

"Not when you fell on me." He looked beyond her and mumbled, "What hurt is you thinking I'm a con man and a cheat."

He looked so crushed, guilt slammed into Rachel's stomach with the force of a speeding bowling ball. "I didn't mean that." At his reproachful glance, she amended her statement. "I guess maybe I sorta did imply something like that."

"You said some pretty cruel things. You hurt my feelings."

"Nicholas, I'm sorry, I—" Rachel froze. "You're doing it again. Manipulating me."

Nicholas snaked his good arm around her shoulders. His eyes laughed at her. "You're too easy, Teach. Your soft spot isn't pride in your strength. Your soft spot is your soft heart."

"My soft head, you mean," she said bitterly. "My determination to clear my father's name is all a big joke to you, isn't it? You've been making fun of me since we met. My hair, my jewelry. My fear of water."

"I never made fun—"

"Forget it. I don't care." She attempted to stand, but his grip turned to steel. "Let go of me. You've made your point." Coming here had been a horrible mistake. Not only had she failed to clear her father, she'd met Nicholas.

"You haven't shut up long enough for me to make my point."

"The point is, you win. Not about my dad. He was innocent, and I intend to prove it. I don't need your help." She wouldn't, couldn't, be another woman in his collection. As if he wanted her to be. "You win about me leaving. As soon as I pack." She didn't need Nicholas Bonelli. She didn't need anyone. Her mother had taught her well.

After her father's death, her mother had refused all offers of help. Rachel had broken down and sobbed when they'd had to leave their home because her mother couldn't afford the mortgage payments on her salary. Mrs. Stuart had turned on her, calling Rachel a selfish sissy who cried when she was losing nothing but a bigger bedroom. Later her mother had fiercely hugged her and said she was sorry, but Rachel never forgot the message. Tears were for sad movies and books but never ever because one was weak enough to feel sorry for herself.

Maybe there were dark moments when she envied others the freedom to be weak. A couple of times she'd even thought it would be nice to lean on someone. She never did. Rachel wasn't a leaner. She tried to remove Nicholas' weighty arm from her shoulders.

"Relax. You're not going anywhere."

"I told you. I'm leaving." The rage within her grew to mammoth proportions. "You shouldn't have told me you'd do it." He shouldn't have made her start to like him. "I hate people who say one thing and mean another. You telling me you'd investigate. Your father telling me he'd answer my questions. Even I lied to me. Telling myself I could clear my father." Telling herself Nicholas's kisses meant something.

"I'm a stupid little nobody who's spent the last fifteen years knowing she has to clear her father. I'm no closer to clearing his name than I am to swimming across that darned lake. I'm a big fat failure. I hate failing." No wonder Nicholas couldn't like her. An angry, renegade tear slipped through her defenses and ran down her cheek.

"Stop it, damn it. You know I hate to see females cry."

"I'm not crying." She swiped at her face. "It only happens when I'm furious."

Nicholas wrapped a curl around his finger. "It's the red hair."

"It has nothing to do with my hair. I'm sick and tired of people assuming I have a bad temper because my hair is red. I don't have any more of a temper than a blonde or a brunette or a bald person. Hair color has nothing to do with temperament. You're just looking for another excuse to make fun of me."

He pulled on her curl as she made to rise. "You're not going anywhere until we get a few things straight between us. Yes, I've teased you about your jewelry, and I've teased you about your total lack of discipline with Scotty, but I have never made fun of your fear of water. As for your hair..." He pressed his fingers against her scalp, turning her face toward his. "I'm fascinated by it, not amused by it."

Looking in his eyes was a major mistake. She didn't want to believe him, but he did sincerity so well. And that other thing. The thing which simmered in the back of his eyes and made her insides go all squishy. "Stop it, Nicholas. Quit trying to flatter me."

"All right."

A sharp pang of disappointment told her she'd hoped for another response from him. "I know you don't like red hair. I'm a carrottop, a clown, a—"

"Woman who talks too much."

Rachel wasn't quite clear how it happened, but suddenly she was on her back on the sofa, Nicholas sprawled on top her. She opened her mouth to object.

Nicholas took advantage of her parted lips.

He never played fair. Kissing her when she hated him. Gingerly she encircled his waist with her arms. He was a no-good cheater, a manipulator, a con man... Through his shirt, she felt his strength, his wiry toughness. His bound arm pressed lightly against the tips of her breasts. Exquisite sensations poured through her veins. Already he'd learned how to pleasure her lips, her mouth, her tongue. Heat built up within her.

"You're as willful as your hair," he muttered against her mouth.

One couldn't push an injured man off the sofa. It wouldn't kill her to kiss him. She loved the taste of his mouth.

Eventually Nicholas raised his head. "Warm heart, sizzling mouth and incandescent hair. They add up to a lethal combination." He toyed with one of her curls. "I've never touched hair like yours. It's like little coiled springs which wrap around a man's fingers and won't let go."

His smiles were lethal. There ought to be a law against them. His breathing—or hers—sounded loud in her ears. He smelled of soap and aftershave.

"I like kissing you," he said.

"I don't like kissing you," she lied. "And I don't like you." After he was whole again, she should seek him out and smash him over the head with a baseball bat. Except she never wanted to see Nicholas Bonelli again for the rest of her life.

Nicholas's muscles flexed as he levered his body off Rachel, moving to the inside of the sofa where he balanced on his uninjured side, facing her. He carefully maneuvered his ankle cast over her legs, pinning her down.

Not that she couldn't escape if she wanted, but it didn't seem quite fair taking advantage of his injuries. His body heat warmed her side from head to toe. She crossed her arms over her chest and glared at him. "Well?"

He raised a mocking brow. "Do your students shiver in their shoes when you give them that fierce, mean look?"

"I don't believe in using fear and intimidation to keep kids in line."

"Just me, huh?"

"Why not? It works so well."

At her sarcastic tone, a crooked smile played over his mouth. "You don't quit, do you?"

"To the contrary. You just called me a quitter, remember? I'm quitting this job. Quitting baby-sitting with you. Quitting counting on you."

"You're not quitting anything," Nicholas said easily.

"Who's stopping me?"

"Me."

"You and what army? You're so staved up, you couldn't stop a newborn baby from rolling over."

"You're right." He gave her a pitiful look. "You can't abandon me. How will I manage?"

"Use your left hand to dial the phone and summon one of your harem up here."

"If I'm in such bad shape that I couldn't keep a baby from rolling over, there's no way I could cope until someone drove up here." He shook his head. "It's a sad commentary on our educational system when a teacher is so illogical."

Her stomach dipped. Not at his words. At the teasing lights in brown eyes and at the lazy masculine satisfaction radiating from him. He was a treacherous, deceiving, manipulative, devastating, self-serving, senses-stirring male.

She wished he'd kiss her again.

Rachel bolted from the sofa. If her last thought hadn't panicked her, she might have felt a tiny twinge of guilt at the wince on his face as his injured leg bounced against the cushions. Instead, she thought only of escape.

She didn't want his kisses. She wanted... She didn't know what she wanted. She'd come to Grand Lake knowing what she'd wanted. Nicholas had confused her with his kisses. She wanted to go home. "I'm going home. I'm leaving today."

"Fine. We'll leave together."

"I am not taking you with me."

"Slow down," Nicholas said.

"Don't tell me how to drive. If driving over Trail Ridge Road scares you, you shouldn't have come. Tell me again why you did come, other than because you're a giant pain in the neck."

"Don't whine. Why don't you get it through that curly red head of yours, you hired me to do a job and I'm doing it."

"I fired you."

"Do you have any idea how frustrating it was when I kept firing you and you wouldn't go away?" He laughed. "You will."

A Clark's nutcracker flew across the road, his white wing patches flashing in the afternoon sun. The gray, black and white bird landed on an old snag at the edge of timberline and surveyed the half dozen elk dozing peacefully in the sunbathed meadow below him. The steep road curved, leaving the pastoral scene behind. In the car, Nicholas's last words lingered.

"Why?" Rachel blurted. "Why do you persist in carrying on with this pretense?" She knew it had nothing to do with wanting to be with her. "We both know you believe your father and you're not going to clear my father.''

''If I said I liked apples, would you assume I disliked oranges?''

''Of course not.''

''Then why do you assume because I believe my father that I'm not going to help you learn the truth about your father?''

Rachel gripped the steering wheel. ''You can't have it both ways.''

''That's where you're wrong. One of the many areas where you're wrong,'' he added dryly. ''People can only tell the truth as they know it. Because my father thinks something is the truth, doesn't mean it is.''

''Nicholas! Are you saying Thane could be guilty without your father knowing it?''

''Damn it, watch the road, Rachel! I don't want to spend the rest of my life wrapped in fiberglass casts.''

''Sorry.'' She waited a second. ''Well, are you?''

''I'm saying I don't know what happened. I'm not out to prove your or anyone else's pet theory. I'm interested in the truth. There is more than one possible explanation for the few facts we know. Until we find out all the facts, or as many as we can find, we shouldn't leap to conclusions. For all you know, the janitor put the sealed bids in your dad's desk.''

''The janitor? I never considered anyone else.''

Nicholas smirked across the car at her. ''That's why you hired me.''

''I fired you.''

''You can't, and don't hit that deer running across the road.''

''I saw her and why can't I fire you?''

''Because I'm not going to let you. Because it's time you knew the truth. Because I'm good at what I do and I can find out that truth for you. Because when I take on a client, I work for that client, not for my father, not for the police department, not for anyone else. And finally, because I have never ever had a client fire me because she didn't trust me. And I sure as hell am not going to let some hot-tempered redhead with kissable lips and a suspicious nature be the first." He added flatly, "Call it professional pride. And watch the damn road. It's curvier here than your hair."

"Quit criticizing my driving. And my hair."

"You're confusing criticism and facts. The road curves. Your hair curls. Your driving stinks. Those aren't criticisms. They're facts."

She refused to acknowledge any of his comments. She might never speak to him again. Then let him try to insist she was his client. If he treated all his clients the way he treated her, he'd be on the breadline in a month. She mentally snorted. "Kissable lips."

"What can I say? I deal in facts. Cute blush."

She hadn't meant to say the words out loud. "Since it appears you won't go away, I think we should keep our relationship strictly business."

"You got it, Teach. Strictly business." Several miles down the road he spoke again. Only this time in a serious tone. "That may be the one thing you're right about. You're the first client I've ever wanted to take to bed. And while the client relationship doesn't exactly preclude my doing just that, sleeping with you would play hell with my objectivity."

"I am not going to sleep with you."

"That's what I said. Why are you shouting at me?"

"I'm not shouting. I'm just sick and tired of hearing about your overactive sex glands." Out of the corner of her eye, she saw Nicholas open his mouth, then snap it closed. Giving her a dark look, he slumped down in his seat. Rachel hummed all the way to Estes Park, where she turned south for Colorado Springs. She'd finally gotten in the last word.

The walk through the police station took forever as person after person waylaid Nicholas to quiz him about the vehicular assault and commiserate with his injuries. Rachel stood circumspectly to the rear as they laughed and joked with him. Occasionally Nicholas remembered her presence and brusquely introduced her. She was in no hurry. Now that the moment had arrived, qualms and second thoughts roiled her stomach.

They turned a corner, moving down another hallway. "C'mon," Nicholas said impatiently. "We'll never get there if you don't quit dawdling."

"Me? I'm not the one getting the ticker tape parade."

He gave her a dry look. "Normally when I drop by to see Dad, I'm lucky to get a wave. Not one person here gives a damn about my injuries. That's an excuse to get an introduction to you. I don't know why you had to bathe in perfume before you came."

"I'm not wearing perfume," Rachel said indignantly, "and I think you ought to give them credit for being interested in your health." She followed him around another corner.

"Their only interest is in you and whether you're sleeping with me." He chuckled. "I'm beginning to think you can turn that blush on and off like a flashing neon light."

"Didn't your mother ever tell you you shouldn't tease a person about physical appearance?" She'd ignore the rest of his comments.

"I suppose that means I'm not supposed to mention the freckles, either? Or the corkscrew curls? Can I say your necklace is, uh, interesting?" He held open a door for her.

Rachel involuntarily reached up and closed her hand

over the giant golf tee hanging around her neck. "It was on my father's key chain. My mother made it into a pendant for me." She wore the pendant when she needed a boost of courage.

"Your father was an avid golfer."

Rachel blinked. Lt. Bonelli stood behind a desk smiling warily at her. "Oh. Hello. I didn't know we were, that is, Nicholas was harassing me and…" Harassing her deliberately, she belatedly realized, because he'd sensed her nervousness. She flashed him a grateful smile.

"Dad asked if you play."

"Play what?"

"Golf," Nicholas said. "I'm still an invalid. Do you think we could sit down?" he asked plaintively.

Rachel dropped into the nearest chair. "No." At Lt. Bonelli's startled look, she said, "I mean, I don't play golf." She had to pull herself together or she'd never be able to deal with whatever tricks Lt. Bonelli intended to pull out of his policeman's hat. "Do you?" She mentally groaned. Of all the lame questions. She didn't care two cents if he played golf or jacks or anything else.

Nicholas reached over and squeezed her shoulder. "Listen, Dollface, me and you came to hear the copper's yarn, so quit acting like a dope and let him shoot the works."

"What?" Rachel and Lt. Bonelli asked in unison.

"You sound like a bad movie," his father added.

Nicholas shrugged. "When your partner locks you out of your office because of a little injury or two, and you're too drugged on painkillers to read, you watch old movies."

"Next time watch musicals," Lt. Bonelli advised.

Nicholas's nonsense had given Rachel time to compose herself. Gripping her purse in her lap, she looked directly at the man who'd killed her father. "I'm here to read that so-called confession."

Lt. Bonelli reached into his desk drawer and pulled out his pipe. He tapped it on the desktop a couple of times. "This is kind of awkward, but the file on your father has disappeared. Probably been misplaced. Fifteen years ago...before computers..." He glanced quickly at Nicholas, then concentrated on running his finger around the bowl of his pipe. "It's around here somewhere. Just a matter of time before it shows up."

Rachel didn't look at Nicholas. His father was lying. Nicholas had to know. His betrayal stabbed deep. She stared down at her purse, trying to convince herself she didn't care. Did Nicholas expect her to say something? What was she supposed to say? Thanks for nothing? Thanks for making me think we could be friends?

She twisted her purse. And realized how close she'd come to betraying her father. If Lt. Bonelli had shown her anything, she would have accepted it. Not because she would have believed it. Self-loathing flooded through her as she faced the truth. Because of Nicholas.

"That's that, then," Nicholas said. "You'll notify us when you find it?"

"Of course," his father heartily agreed, standing in dismissal.

Rachel had no intention of leaving. Nicholas must think she had the brains of dead gnat. "I'm not—"

"Going to bother my dad anymore," Nicholas interposed.

She turned toward him, opening her mouth to argue, then pressed her lips together at the commanding stare he gave her. His eyes slid toward the door in an unmistakable message. After a second, Rachel rose slowly from her chair and walked out of Lt. Bonelli's office. She could always return. Behind her Nicholas told his dad they were going next to Robert Thane's office.

The minute Nicholas closed the door to his father's

office, Rachel rounded on him. "What happened to working for—"

Nicholas's hard kiss cut off her angry question. "Be quiet," he muttered against her lips. Then he craned his head against the door, listening intently to something on the other side. His eyes narrowed thoughtfully.

"What?" Rachel whispered.

Another hard kiss answered her. She felt the door behind Nicholas open.

"I thought you'd left," Lt. Bonelli said.

Rachel jerked away from Nicholas. Heat rose to her cheeks.

Nicholas brushed his thumb over one fiery cheek, a crooked smile on his mouth. "I got distracted." He gave Rachel a long, steady look. A look of warning.

Whirling away, she practically sprinted to the connecting hallway.

"What's going on with you and that woman?" Nicholas' father demanded, his voice carrying around the corner. "First she's hired to help you, without my knowledge, I might add, or I would have advised against it. Then she's supposedly your client trying to dig up something better left buried. And now she's kissing you in the hallway."

"Correction. I was kissing her."

"Find a better place to do it," Lt. Bonelli snapped.

Nicholas laughed. "C'mon, Dad. Any place is a good place to kiss an attractive woman."

Rachel had no idea where she was. Coming in she'd paid too little attention to the hallways Nicholas had led her through.

Nicholas. If he thought calling her an attractive woman would turn her into a mindless robot, he'd find out how wrong he could be. Anger and hurt battled within her, first one emotion winning, then the other. How dare Nicholas pretend his father's flimsy excuse had even the slightest hint of truth about it? The way he'd hustled her out of there angered. The way he'd silenced her with a kiss stung. He couldn't have shown his contempt for her more clearly if he'd called her "that woman" as his father had. "That woman." As if she had a communicable disease.

Or a past. As if she were the daughter of a criminal. The son of a cop would never be interested in a criminal's daughter.

Rachel walked faster, ignoring Nicholas as he limped to catch up with her.

A tall, well-groomed brunette came around the corner. "Nick!" she said in delight. Shifting her leather briefcase to her other hand, the woman raised her face for Nicholas's kiss. "I didn't know you were back in town."

Nicholas caught Rachel's arm when she would have continued down the hall. "I returned yesterday. Still catching up."

The woman looked at Rachel and raised an elegant eyebrow. "So I see."

"She's a client. Summer James. Rachel Stuart. If you ever need a criminal attorney, Rachel, call Summer. She's one of the best. Gotta run, Summer, have an appointment."

The woman's crisp request for Nicholas to call her followed them down the hall.

Rachel shook off the hand gripping her arm. "I've had enough of these stupid games you and your father are playing."

"Don't get in a pet, sister. Me and you got to beat it over to Thane's joint." He grinned at her.

"I'm not amused, and you're fired."

"Swell," Nicholas said absently.

"Did you hear me? You're fired."

Nicholas's eyes narrowed to thin slits. "There's something strange going on."

"Yeah," Rachel retorted. "Armed invaders from Mars."

"Besides that."

Rachel gave up. You couldn't fire a man who was so lost in a brown study he didn't even know he'd been fired.

Outside the police station, Nicholas headed away from Rachel's car, saying he wanted to walk. Even slowed by the walking cast on his ankle, they'd almost reached the tall office building near the old Alamo Building before Nicholas spoke again. "Why didn't he want you to see the confession?" he mused as they waited for the traffic light to turn green.

"You mean, you didn't believe him?" When he didn't respond, she jabbed him in his good side with her elbow. "Nicholas!"

"What?"

"Remember me? Your client?"

"I thought you fired me."

She gave him an exasperated glare. "If you heard me fire you, why are we standing here?"

The walk signal came on and Nicholas took off. "I'm going to sniff around Thane and see if I can figure out what's going on. Since I don't have a gun pointed at you, I guess you're going along because you didn't really mean it about firing me."

Rachel held open the heavy glass door. "I meant it. I'm going because I have my own questions to ask." She scowled at him. "If I'm allowed to talk, that is."

Nicholas pushed the elevator button. "Of course you're allowed to talk. Why wouldn't you be?"

"How would I know? You're the one who's always shutting me up by kissing me." The last three words came out louder than she'd intended. Two men walking past the elevator looked at her and Nicholas with interest. Rachel's face flamed. The elevator doors slid open and she rushed to enter.

As they traveled upward, Rachel starred at the numbers over the door, conscious of Nicholas at her side. His soap smelled of sandalwood and a hint of something herbal. A gift from one of his lady friends. Or maybe JoJo. Soap would be the kind of gift a young niece would love to give her uncle. And Nicholas was the kind of uncle who would use the soap, knowing it pleased JoJo.

Rachel had bought her father sandalwood shower soap for Christmas one year. After his death, her mother had given the unused soap to the same charity who'd collected his worn clothing. Her father had used plain-smelling soap from the grocery store. Until shortly before he died when he began smelling somehow exotic. When Rachel had commented on his new smell, he'd told her people needed to occasionally add little pleasures to their humdrum lives. Like root beer floats, she'd said, and he had laughed. Her mother, who was always worried about too much sugar in her family's diet, had laughed, too, but not as heartily.

The elevator stopped and the doors silently opened. Rachel took a deep breath. Fifteen years ago Parker and Thane had occupied much less luxurious quarters. Here the marble walls and plush carpeting shouted of money.

Nicholas nudged her. "Let's go. Unless you've changed your mind."

"I haven't changed anything." She exited the elevator.

He squeezed her shoulders. "That's my girl."

"I'm not your girl. And I'm not 'that woman.'"

He understood at once. "Dad didn't mean anything by it."

"Of course he did. He meant I'm the daughter of a crook."

"What if you are?"

"I'm not."

"It doesn't matter then, does it?" He guided her around the corner toward a set of open double glass doors. "Even if you are, it doesn't matter."

Not to him. Because she meant nothing to him. "It matters to me. I don't like anyone thinking of me as 'that woman.'"

"I don't think of you that way." Nicholas gave her a slow, lazy smile. "I think of you as that redheaded woman."

CHAPTER NINE

"NICHOLAS," Rachel began furiously, "I swear I— "

"Mr. Bonelli? And this must be little Rachel."

Rachel spun around. A portly, middle-aged man walked quickly across the wide expanse of gray-carpeted floor in the reception area. Rachel ignored his hand stuck out in welcome. Robert Thane was older and heavier, but she would have recognized him anywhere. Parker and Thane had always hosted family Christmas parties. Maybe they still did. He shook hands with Nicholas. She couldn't help but contrast the two men. Nicholas in his charcoal, pin-striped suit looked more the part of the CEO of a major company than did Robert Thane in his rumpled tan slacks and rolled-up shirtsleeves.

Thane smiled tentatively at her, and didn't repeat the mistake of extending his hand. "It's been a long time, Rachel. You've turned into quite an attractive young woman. I always thought you would. How's your mother and Tony?"

She clutched her purse in front of her with both hands. "I'm not here for a social visit, Mr. Thane. Nicholas, Mr. Bonelli, said you'd agreed to talk to me about the crime my father is theoretically supposed to have committed." She didn't think she imagined the way Thane's face tightened at her words.

"You didn't have to hire a private detective, Rachel. I would have talked to you anytime you wanted." He led the way into a well-appointed office and showed Rachel to one of a pair of maroon leather chairs.

She sat in the other chair. Nicholas silently sat in the chair Rachel had rejected.

Thane went around his huge desk and sat, gazing steadily at Rachel. "What do you want to know?"

"I want to know why you framed my father."

Thane leaned back in his chair, tenting his hands in front of his chin. "Is that what your mother told you?"

"She said my father didn't do it. Not that Tony or I needed her to tell us that. I figured out by myself that you framed him."

Thane glanced at Nicholas. "Not from you?"

"No," Nicholas said calmly.

"Nicholas is here because he thinks I'm trying to pin the crime on his father."

Thane looked back at Nicholas. "I was under the impression you were working for Rachel."

"She fired me."

"So you are here representing your father's interests?"

"I'm here to see Rachel finds her answers."

"I see." Thane closed his eyes in a posture of contemplation. He tapped his lower lip with his fingers.

The tension inside Rachel grew almost unbearable. Despite a breathtaking view of downtown Colorado Springs with Pikes Peak in the background, the room pressed in on her. Huge expanses of fixed glass isolated the three people in the office from the outside air and the noise and odor of cars moving along the streets far below. A pigeon flapping silently past the window seemed somehow surreal. Rachel wanted to throw something through Thane's window. She wanted to escape.

She wanted Nicholas to take her hand. To drag her away. To kiss her. To tell her it didn't matter whether her father was a crook. Except it did matter. Not to Nicholas. He wouldn't care if a client of his was related to a criminal or a bishop. She was nothing but a client to him. His redheaded client.

Thane opened his eyes and gave Nicholas a questioning look. "I suppose your dad told you two about the bank account and Marv's confession."

"You know he did," Nicholas said.

At the same time, Rachel said, "I don't believe it."

Thane sighed. "Marvin Stuart worked with me for fourteen years. He was smart, creative, had an eye for details. Saw things I missed. I considered him a friend as well as an employee." He hesitated. "My grandfather and Parker were partners who found a rich vein of gold in Cripple Creek in the 1890s. Parker was a mason and my grandfather a boat builder. They didn't know a thing about mining, so they sold out and settled in Colorado Springs where they did what they knew. They built things."

"I know the history of the company," Rachel said. "I want to know why you accused my father of a crime he didn't commit."

"The papers in his desk—"

"Could have been there for any number of reasons."

"You have to understand it all happened so fast. We found the papers, then the bank account. When we asked your father about them, he readily confessed to selling the information in the sealed bids. I expected an explanation, not that, not from an old friend. He insisted on writing a confession then and there. Later we went to the bank and he turned the money over to me. I was in shock. He asked to be allowed to go home and explain to your mother. I thought he'd left long before the police. When someone came running in and said Marv had stepped in front of a police car... That had to be the blackest, longest day of my life. Marv was my friend. My wife and I used to play bridge with him and Gail."

"But you believed he'd cheat and steal."

"At first. After the shock wore off, I began thinking." He picked up a pencil from his cluttered desktop and bounced it against a book. "I think he was covering for someone else."

"Did you share your suspicions with the police?" Nicholas asked.

Thane swiveled his chair around so he faced the window. "No," he said over his shoulder. "I was too ashamed. Marv was a friend and I'd let him down by believing he'd betrayed me."

"So you let everyone go on thinking he was guilty," Rachel said bitterly.

"I hired a private detective to look into it." Thane half turned toward her. "Whoever sold the information in the sealed bids covered his trail too well. The guy found nothing."

"Who'd you hire?" Nicholas asked.

Thane flapped his hand. "Some guy. I forget his name. He's not in town anymore. Can't remember where he went."

Rachel's knuckles were white in her lap. "And that's it? You tell a woman her husband and the father of their children is a criminal, and then when you decide he's not, you don't bother to tell her that?"

Gripping the arms of his chair, his eyes blinking rapidly, the older man faced Rachel. "It's no excuse, but I felt so damned guilty. I wanted to forget the whole thing. I justified my actions by telling myself the whole thing had been hushed up when your dad died. No one knew, so I figured no harm done. I don't know why your mom told you. Your brother know, too?"

"Tony knows about the accusations. None of us knew you'd changed your mind about my father's guilt."

Nicholas stirred. "He didn't say that. He said he thought your dad might have been covering for someone else."

Thane's gaze darted over to Nicholas and back to Rachel. "I can't prove it, but I'm convinced Marv was innocent." His voice strengthened. "I'm positive he wasn't guilty."

"And his death?" Rachel asked in a brittle voice.

"A ghastly, horrible accident. Definitely an accident. No doubt about that. Your dad was distraught. Knowing someone had framed him. And me, his friend, believing Marv could betray me." Thane looked steadily at Rachel. "He stepped into the street without looking. It was an accident. There was no way for Bonelli to stop in time." He turned to Nicholas. "Your dad attempted CPR long past all hope. The ambulance guys had to pull him off Marv."

"She's not little Rachel anymore," Nicholas said obliquely. "She can handle the truth. She's tough."

Thane slid his hands off his desk and scooted his chair forward. "That is the truth," he said earnestly.

Nicholas stood up abruptly. "Let's get out of here."

"Yes." She stumbled to her feet. Her father was innocent, and this man had known it. And never told them. She couldn't forgive his cruelty.

Despite his ankle cast, Nicholas beat her to the elevator and hit the call button.

"Thank you, Nicholas. I don't think he would have told me the truth without you. He must have realized the detective he hired was no good. Knowing your reputation, he knew you'd find out the truth." She swallowed hard. "After all this time, to find out my father didn't do it. I mean, I knew he didn't, but to have proof." She wasn't a criminal's daughter. Rachel smiled mistily up at Nicholas.

He stared back in amazement. "Don't tell me you believe those lies he tossed around in there?"

"What lies?" She'd hoped Nicholas hadn't noticed.

"C'mon, Rachel. Didn't you notice the way his eyes

kept sliding away from us? All that blinking. A first year criminology student could see he was lying through his teeth.''

She followed him into the elevator. ''You're just guessing. It might have been an accident. Forget it. I am.''

Reaching toward the elevator buttons, Nicholas froze. ''What might have been an accident?'' he asked in an icy voice. ''Are you referring to your father's death?''

''It was obvious. His overemphasis on how it was an accident.'' She tentatively touched his arm. ''Mr. Thane could be wrong about that part. I'm not going to pursue it.''

''I do not believe my father deliberately ran your father down.'' Nicholas savagely punched the ground floor button. ''Any more than I believe that fairy tale about your father covering for someone.''

''Fairy tale!'' Red spots of rage danced a war dance across Rachel's field of vision. ''It's not a question of your dad or mine,'' she said furiously. ''Why can't they both be innocent?''

''That was a clever touch. Not pitting us against each other. The anonymous third person.''

''I hate you, Nicholas.'' The lump in her throat swelled to overwhelming proportions. She'd gotten what she wanted, her father's name cleared. She ought to be thrilled. Why did she feel so empty? ''You never wanted to help me. You're saying my dad was guilty because...'' She couldn't figure out why. It made no sense. Unless. ''I didn't realize how much you resented needing my help up in Grand Lake,'' she said slowly.

''I have two choices here,'' Nicholas said through his teeth. ''I can ignore what you're implying or I can make you take it back.''

''You can't make me anything, Nicholas Bonelli.'' She backed up as he stalked her across the small elevator. "I fired you. You and I are quits." Her spine hit the wall of the elevator.

Nicholas crowded up against her. He stuck his left hand under her chin, forcing her head up. "Quits, Teach? I don't think so." He rubbed his thumb back and forth across her chin. "You wanted the truth, remember?"

"I have the truth."

"I'm beginning to think you wouldn't know the truth if it smacked you on the mouth." His eyes darkened. "Or did this."

"Don't you dare kiss me, Nicholas Bo—" Her resistance melted in the heat of his kiss. Nicholas kissed better than any man who'd ever kissed her. This would be the last time he kissed her, and she wanted the kiss to be one she'd never regret. Which meant throwing herself wholeheartedly into it.

A faint hissing noise sounded behind Nicholas. "Ground floor. Are you getting out?" a voice inquired politely.

"No," Nicholas said. "Take another elevator." Reaching over, he jabbed the button to close the door.

"You can't do that," Rachel said.

"The hell I can't." He sent the elevator winging skyward again. "Now, where were we?"

"On the ground floor."

His eyes laughed at her. "Not anymore." He trailed a finger over her bottom lip. "I got jealous every time you let Scotty do this." Leaning down, he slowly drew his tongue across her mouth.

The fast-rising elevator played havoc with Rachel's stomach. "I never let him," she said breathlessly. "I hated it." She didn't hate Nicholas doing it. Her lips parted.

"I like your hair down," he muttered.

Her hair, released from the smart twist she'd put it up

in earlier, fell to her shoulders, brushing the sensitive hairs on her neck in passing. He wove his fingers into the thick mass. "You smell like some kind of exotic flower." He dropped tiny kisses randomly across her face and neck until he found her earlobe. "You have a cute little freckle here." In a louder voice, he said, "This one's occupied. Use one of the others."

The elevator door swished closed again and the elevator swooped downward. "Nicholas, we have to get off this elevator before they call the police."

"Don't worry your pretty little red head about that, Teach." He slid his hand around behind her. "A kiss from you is worth being sent up the river for."

"Your father's right." She could scarcely breathe as Nicholas investigated her spine, vertebra by vertebra, working his way leisurely down her back. "You've been watching too much TV." He hadn't seen this maneuver on television. One by one her bones dissolved at his touch. The weakness spread downward, liquefying her knees. Impossible to move even if the elevator door had opened again. She clutched Nicholas around his neck.

He barely turned his head. "This elevator's out of order."

The door closed with barely a whisper of a sound. Rachel ducked her head into the crook of his neck and breathed deeply of sandalwood scent. "We can't ride up and down all day."

"Why not?"

"Because..." There had to be some reason. "Because." His raised eyebrow told her he wanted more of a reason. Her mind refused to cooperate. "Because I said so."

Nicholas laughed softly. "You sound like my mother."

Mother. Rachel stared at him in horror. How could she have forgotten her mother? She should be rushing home to tell her mother what Robert Thane had said. Mrs. Stuart had always believed her husband innocent, and now Robert Thane admitted he knew it, too. Her mother could once again hold her head up. She could if she knew about it. Which she didn't because Rachel was playing games in the elevator. With a man who didn't believe Robert Thane. Who didn't believe in her father's innocence. Rachel stiffened and pressed against the elevator, striving to put distance between her and Nicholas.

He gave her a crooked smile. "I take it recess is over."

Rachel put as much coldness in her voice as she could. "It's all over. I found out what I wanted to know."

"It's not over."

Rachel stuck her nose in the air, refusing to speak to him. The elevator descended once more to the ground floor. The opening door framed two uniformed policemen.

Nicholas nodded. "Hello, Tom, Walt. What brings you guys here?"

"Complaints about some nuts riding this elevator. We're clearing the lobby in case they're dangerous. You happen to see which way the guys who were in this elevator went?"

Nicholas held out his good hand. "Slap on the cuffs. I'm your hijacker. My client needed a little privacy after hearing some distressing news. Since there's a whole bank of elevators, I saw no problem suggesting a few people ride one of the others. Sorry, guys." Nicholas smiled sheepishly. "Dad's going to have my head over this."

The policemen laughed. One slapped Nicholas on the back and went out to disperse the crowd milling about on the sidewalk. The other shook his head. "Better you on the carpet with the lieutenant than me. Heard about your injuries." He cast a sideways glance at Rachel. "Guess there are tradeoffs in your business. Danger versus women. You've always got a beautiful woman on your arm. Maybe I ought to think about being a private cop so I can get some of those women."

"You're married, Tom."

"Yeah," the cop said. "Two kids. Why couldn't I have been smart like you?"

"Dumb like me, you mean," Nicholas said. "A man with a wife and two kids has pretty much got it all. I envy you."

"Yeah, right." The cop gave a casual wave and walked off.

"Smart like you," Rachel said in disgust as they exited the building to the stares of the returning crowd. "What's so smart about throwing an entire building into a frenzy? If you'd been anybody else, they'd have tossed you in jail and thrown away the key."

"I remember Tom getting married." Nicholas's thoughts had taken a different road from Rachel's. "Doesn't seem that long ago, yet the lucky son of a gun has two kids. And look at Charlie. One day we're nineteen. The next he has Dyan and Andy and JoJo. Makes a man wonder how and why he missed the boat."

"We both know you have no intention of giving up your bachelor life. You're not the type to trade all those Bunnies and Summers for falling asleep in front of the TV or changing diapers, so drop the pathetic act. I don't feel sorry for you." She walked faster.

Even limping, Nicholas kept pace. "What time does your mother get off work?"

"What business is that of yours?"

"You'll have to wait until she gets home to tell her what Thane said. We'll pick up some take-out food since she won't be expecting us."

Whirling, Rachel faced Nicholas in the middle of the

street. "You're not going to my mother's house with me."

Taking her arm, Nicholas propelled her in the direction of her car. "I'm beginning to think she can clear up a few things."

"My mother has nothing to clear up, and you are not going to her house. The last thing she wants to do is meet the son of the man who killed her husband."

"You heard Thane. It was an accident."

"It's much easier to believe my dad is a crook than that your dad is a murderer, isn't it?"

Nicholas grabbed her purse. "Maybe if you called my dad and yours 'X' and 'Y,' it would be easier for you to see the facts staring you in the face." He unlocked the passenger door with her car keys before tossing the key ring to her.

"I can see all the facts I need to see." Rachel walked around to the driver's side and slid behind the wheel. "I can see that you are determined to call my dad a crook. Mr. Thane absolved your dad of any guilt in my dad's death. Why can't you let the whole thing go?"

"You hired me to find out the truth. What kind of food does your mother like? Where should we go for pickup?"

"You are not going to my mother's house, and that's final."

Rachel slammed the little white boxes of Chinese food on her mother's kitchen table. "I'm not going to tell my mother who you are and why you're here. You horned your way in, you can darned well explain your rude intrusion to her. I don't even know why you're here. And don't give me that garbage about finding out the truth. I know the truth now, and so do you."

"The truth about what?"

Rachel spun around. "Mother! I didn't hear you come in."

"I noticed. You were too busy arguing with your friend."

"He's no friend," Rachel snapped.

"Mrs. Stuart, I'm Nick Bonelli, of Addison and Bonelli, Security and Investigations."

"Bonelli." Mrs. Stuart turned ghastly white and her knees started to buckle.

Catching her before she fell, Nicholas helped her to a chair.

"I told you not to come. I didn't want him to come, Mother, but he always thinks he knows better."

"Bonelli. Any relation to a policeman named Bonelli?"

"He's my father."

"Rachel?" her mother appealed. "I don't understand what's going on. I thought you were up in Grand Lake helping out a fellow teacher by taking care of her invalid brother."

"I came back yesterday." Rachel felt her cheeks turn red under her mother's accusing stare. "I didn't exactly tell you the whole story, Mother."

"I'm the invalid," Nicholas interposed. "I was injured when a car hit me. Rachel's been my, uh—"

"Baby-sitter," she snapped, "and you've been acting like a baby, always having to have your own way."

"You've been up at Grand Lake with this man? Just the two of you? When you said a teacher's brother, I thought you meant a teenager or something, at least, that was my impression..."

Rachel's face color intensified. She knew exactly where her mother had gotten that impression. "I may have fudged a little," she admitted, "but I couldn't tell you the whole thing."

"You're an adult, Rachel. You don't need to explain." Mrs. Stuart paused. "You said the injured person was the brother of your friend, Dyan. Was that fudging, too?"

"Dyan's my sister," Nicholas said.

"Another Bonelli. Did you know that, Rachel? From your face, I see you did," Mrs. Stuart said slowly. She closed her eyes. "Why, Rachel? Why couldn't you leave it be?"

"It's not fair to hide the truth from her."

"You don't know what you're talking about," Rachel's mother said wearily, resting her forehead on her hand.

"I know Rachel's a grown woman with courage and strength. You don't need to protect her anymore."

"She loved her father so much."

"As I'm sure you did," Nicholas said. "You survived. Do you really think Rachel is weak?"

"Of course she's not weak," Mrs. Stuart snapped. "I brought her up to be strong."

"Then have faith in the way you raised her. Have faith in Rachel. Tell her the truth."

"Knowing the truth isn't always all it's cracked up to be." Mrs. Stuart looked at Rachel. "Knowing who Nicholas Bonelli was, you took the job?" The muscles in her face sagged, aging her. "I see. You took the job *because* of who he was. Why? Did you hope to reach his father through him? For what purpose? Didn't you believe what I told you?"

"She believed you," Nicholas said gently. "She believed too much. She wanted to clear her father."

Mrs. Stuart turned to stare in shock at Nicholas.

He steadily returned her gaze.

"That possibility never occurred to me," she said at last. "It should have. Rachel adored her father."

"As you said yourself, she's an adult now."

They seemed to be talking in a code only they knew

the key to. Rachel shrank within herself. A chill invaded her bones. She felt as if she were teetering on the edge of a dock, overlooking a deep, threatening lake. A lake waiting to suck her into its cold, dark depths. Fear flooded over her. She didn't want to know. She wasn't grown up. She was a scared little girl, hiding her head from the bogeyman. "Never mind," she quickly said to her mother. "I was wrong to start this. I knew it, or I never would have gone behind your back. I'm sorry, Mother." She couldn't look at Nicholas. He could think what he wanted about the times she'd kissed him. It didn't matter now. "You can go home. I found out what I wanted to know."

Mrs. Stuart touched one of the small white cartons piled on the table. "Chinese?"

"Would you like to eat first or talk?" Nicholas asked.

Mrs. Stuart gave him a wry smile. "Do you really think I could choke down food?"

"We'll eat after he leaves," Rachel said. "He insisted on coming. He can get himself home. He can call one of his girlfriends." She gave her mother a glancing look. "He has one for every day of the week and a few to spare."

"You'd better sit down, Mr. Bonelli." Mrs. Stuart nodded at the chair across from her. "I didn't notice the cast on your leg. We can reheat the food later. If you care to stay and eat after I've had my say."

"I don't have to stay," he said. "I don't need the truth. Rachel does."

"Liar. What he wants is for you to tell him his father didn't murder Dad."

"Rachel! Of course his father didn't murder yours. Where did you get such an outrageous idea? Mr. Bonelli, I'm so sorry if anything I said gave Rachel the idea her father was deliberately killed. That is...well, whatever happened, your father was in no way to blame."

"Maybe he didn't mean to run him over," Rachel said tightly, "but his accusations and threats drove Daddy into the street. Mr. Thane said Daddy was so distraught he didn't know what he was doing."

"Robert Thane said that? You talked to him?"

"To him and to Lt. Bonelli," Rachel said defiantly. "Nicholas's father lied. Said they'd lost the file on the case. Mr. Thane said Daddy was covering up for someone. That Daddy didn't do it, that Daddy never would have betrayed a friend."

Mrs. Stuart shook her head slowly. "You were twelve and you idolized your father. I never thought about when you grew up. After the first year, you hardly mentioned him. I had no idea you'd become obsessed with his death."

"It's not obsessed to want to clear your father's name."

"Maybe I should have told you the truth from the beginning." Mrs. Stuart looked at Nicholas. "I wanted to spare her. Was that so wrong?"

Nicholas reached across the table and took Mrs. Stuart's hand. "Loving someone is never wrong. You did what you thought was best."

Mrs. Stuart nodded. "He left me so empty. I had nothing else to give her."

"You gave her a great deal. She's kind, generous, nurturing, determined, brave and tough. She may not look it, but she's got the heart and guts of ten people. As I imagine her mother has."

"I don't deserve that, but thank you." Mrs. Stuart gave him a wobbly smile before turning to her daughter.

"No." Rachel shook her head. "You never lied to me. I know you didn't."

Her mother looked steadily at her. "I'm sorry, Rachel, more sorry than I can say. I should have told you before.'' She paused. ''Mr. Bonelli is right. You've grown up into an individual with strength and courage.''

''He's not right. Send him away. He's stupid, Mother, really he is. He's so stupid he thinks he can't fall in love just because he didn't fall in love by the time he reached puberty. He's dumb. You can't believe anything he says. Tell me you didn't lie to me, Mother, please tell me you didn't lie.''

''He was leaving us,'' her mother said baldly. ''He'd met a woman.''

''I don't believe you.''

''She wouldn't go away with him unless he had money. Lots of money. He sold the only thing he had to sell. The information in the sealed bids.''

''No. No.''

''He betrayed Robert Thane, his employer and his friend,'' Mrs. Stuart continued relentlessly. ''He betrayed the other employees of Parker and Thane. Losing the bidding meant lost jobs. He betrayed me and you and Tony.''

''He didn't betray Mr. Thane. He said Daddy didn't do it. That he was covering for someone.''

''Robert Thane lied to you, Rachel. We used to play cards with the Thanes. We were good friends. Afterward, Robert wanted to help us, but I was too ashamed to accept his help. When he heard what I'd told you, I'm sure he thought lying to you was what I would want. It was his way of helping me. He saw your father once with the woman and blamed himself for not confronting Marv or telling me.''

''No.'' Rachel wanted to press her hands over her ears to block out her mother's lies.

''Yes.'' Mrs. Stuart took a deep breath. ''In the end, your father betrayed his lover and himself. His death was no accident.''

''Mrs. Stuart,'' Nicholas began. ''My father didn't—''

"You wanted me to tell her the truth," Rachel's mother cut in sharply. "I loved her father, but the truth is Marv was weak. She'd have seen it herself if she'd been older. He always made excuses, never blamed himself for anything. I'm sure the police suspected that Marv deliberately walked into the street in front of your father's car, Mr. Bonelli." Her voice caught. "I believe he committed suicide. He simply couldn't face the consequences of what he'd done."

She looked at Nicholas. "If he knew your father was driving, or if he just picked the first car he saw coming... That we'll never know."

"You don't have to say these things to make Nicholas feel better. He's so...so self-righteous he never believed his father killed my father anyway."

"All those times he said he was golfing with clients. The nights he supposedly was working late. New clothes. Going to a hair stylist instead of a barber. New toiletries, soaps. Maybe it was my fault. Maybe I was too wrapped up in the children. I should have paid more attention to Marvin's needs."

"I don't believe you." Waves of pain engulfed Rachel.

"Rachel."

The gentle tone of voice Nicholas used to say her name destroyed any hope Rachel had that her mother was wrong. "I am not the daughter of a crook. I'm not. I won't be." She gave a hysterical giggle. "I'd be just the kind of woman parents want teaching their children, wouldn't I?" Her voice turned unctuous. "You know our Ms. Stuart, don't you? Her father was a common crook who committed suicide when he got caught. She's just the person to teach little Johnny all about values."

"Stop it, Rachel," Nicholas said curtly. "You're getting hysterical and upsetting your mother."

"I'm not hysterical. What's to get hysterical about?

Except for the whole situation. It's hysterical. Hysterically funny. My mother's a liar and my father's a crook and a womanizer. At least you're honest about that, Nicholas. You don't lie about your womanizing.''

"I'm not a womanizer.''

"My father probably said the same thing. Maybe he wasn't. Maybe he just wanted an excuse to leave us.''

"Quit feeling sorry for yourself," Nicholas said.

"You're right. I have nothing to feel sorry for myself about." No man could love a criminal's daughter. Nicholas couldn't. "My life is in tatters, so what?''

"Your life is not in tatters. Your life is exactly what it was. The only thing that has changed is now you know something you didn't know before. Live with it.''

"Thank you, Nicholas Bonelli, for those uplifting words.''

"You're welcome. Let's eat. I'm starving.''

Only an inconsiderate, egotistical, self-centered, insensitive clod could think of his stomach at a time like this. Rachel's stomach revolted at the thought of food. She wanted to scream. She wanted to drop to the floor and pound her feet and fists against the mottled linoleum. She wanted to smash the dinner plates Nicholas was setting on the table. She wanted to throw against the wall the food her mother was so carefully reheating in the microwave. She wanted to howl.

She wouldn't. If they could be so unconcerned about the disaster in her life, so could she. "Parents like their teachers to be above mere mortals, so maybe I should go into a whole new career. I have no idea what that would be. Certainly I couldn't be a bookkeeper or work in a bank because, if my father's crime-ridden life ever came to light, I'd be fired in a millisecond. No one is going to let the daughter of a crook within a million miles of money. The same's true for poor Tony, who's working for a CPA firm but wants to go to law school.

He can forget that. Who wants to hire a crook for a lawyer?''

Rachel snapped her fingers as if struck with inspiration. ''Maybe he can work with your friend, Summer, for the defense. Don't they say it takes a crook to know a crook? He could be a real advantage for her. Her own private lie detector. She could ask a few questions, and Tony would know who was a crook and who wasn't. Except that wouldn't work, would it? Tony thinks his father was an honest man.'' She blanched at the look on her mother's face. ''You told Tony the truth, but not me?''

''He came to me,'' her mother said apologetically, ''a couple of years ago. I thought about telling you then, but you never mentioned Marv, and I couldn't see the need to bring up old hurts.''

''So I'm the only one who didn't know. I feel like the world's biggest chump.'' She turned on Nicholas. ''You knew. You knew all along. You jerk. You miserable, insufferable, mean-spirited jerk. It was all a game to you. Having a little fun with Rachel. You have girlfriends for all your other activities. Oh,'' she said flatly, ''now I understand. In your condition, you couldn't keep up with those women and their gung-ho activities, and you couldn't sleep with them. You were bored, so you used me for entertainment. You must have had an uproarious time laughing and snickering at me. Were Dyan and Charlie in on the joke? Did you wager on how long I'd play the stupid sap? I'm happy I gave you all so much to laugh at. Now get out of my mother's house.''

''Rachel,'' her mother said, ''you're hurting, and I'm sorry. Your father let you down and I let you down. Don't take it out on Mr. Bonelli. Eat and you'll feel better.'' She edged a dish of fried rice toward Rachel.

Rachel swept the tabletop with her outstretched arm. The dish of rice went flying. ''Eating won't make me feel better. Nothing will make me feel better. You lied to me.'' Jumping to her feet, she rushed out of the house.

Ignoring Nicholas's imperious voice calling her, she fumbled to unlock her car door.

''I said, wait a minute.''

''I heard you. Get your own darned ride home. I'm not driving you.''

''That's not what I wanted.'' He hesitated. ''I wanted to ask you to marry me.''

CHAPTER TEN

RACHEL slapped him. Or she would have if Nicholas hadn't caught her hand as it arced toward his face. "Me? Marry you?" She laughed until she cried. Nicholas released her wrist and wrapped his good arm around her shoulders.

She wept all over his expensive suit. Tears of mirth at first, then tears of sorrow. She cried for the grief and the love she'd wasted on a man she never really knew. She cried for her mother and her suffering. Her mother who told Tony the truth, but not Rachel. She cried because she'd found the truth and lost her father. And because Nicholas asked her to marry him when he didn't love her.

Her father hadn't loved her and her mother believed her weak. She was weak. The tears she couldn't stop proved that. She, who'd prided herself on her strength, bawling like a baby. Rachel no longer knew who or what she was. All these years, the things she'd believed in, the people she'd believed in. Her life. All based on a sordid lie.

She used up all her tears, leaving her drained body an empty shell. Her breath came in ragged gulps. Nicholas gently dried her wet cheeks. "I should have listened to you," she said, evading his gaze. Taking the soggy handkerchief he held out, she blew her nose. "You tried to convince me to leave it alone."

Nicholas wrapped one of her curls around his finger. "You accused me of knowing all along. I didn't. I knew Dad was convinced your father committed the crime, but Dad never told me about the other woman."

He didn't mention the other. Her father's suicide. Belatedly Rachel understood Robert Thane's repeated emphasis on her dad's death being an accident. He wasn't lying because of Nicholas's father. He was lying because of Rachel's father. Like Rachel's mother, Robert Thane believed Marvin Stuart had killed himself. Her father was a crook and a suicide.

And Nicholas Bonelli said he wanted to marry her. He couldn't want to marry her. He couldn't love her. It hit her then. "Pity," she said dully. "You're offering to marry me because you feel sorry for me. Poor freckled, redheaded Rachel with her tainted blood. You think no man will marry me once he hears about my father."

"I don't feel sorry for you. I want to marry you."

"Of course," she said slowly. "You and your family think there's something wrong with you because you haven't fallen in love. What better woman to marry than one who's equally flawed."

"You're not flawed. You're—"

"The daughter of a crook, a man who betrayed and abandoned his family for another woman, a man who everyone believes killed himself. Including your father."

"That's it," Nicholas said in startled comprehension. "That's why Dad lied. And why he phoned Thane after we left his office. To tell Thane what he'd told us so their stories matched. Dad deliberately misplaced the file. Up at the lake he made up that tale about your dad doing it for his family. Then when he reviewed the confession, he must have seen a mention of your dad's girlfriend."

Rachel blew her nose again. "Your father didn't like you kissing me. He'd never accept you marrying me. Your family would scratch your name from the family Bible."

"My family is not asking you to marry them. I am. I want to marry you."

A shaft of sun spotlighted the ragged petals of a huge red-orange poppy lying in a forlorn heap at the bottom of a barren stalk. Rachel stared at the petals. She'd never liked poppies. They were too gaudy. Like her hair. The blossom had died. But it would bloom again next year.

A traitorous seed of hope unfurled deep within Rachel's breast. Nicholas said he wanted to marry her. The rest of her life spent with Nicholas. Smiling at her. Arguing with her. Laughing with her. A house filled with good times and pets and children. His children. Children with black curly hair, dark chocolate brown eyes. She almost smiled. Maybe a redhead thrown in to mix things up. A house filled with love. Her half-formed vision dissolved. Nicholas had said nothing about love. She took a deep breath. "Why do you want to marry me?"

"I want a wife, kids, a home life. When I was describing you to your mother, it hit me. I want to get married, and you fit the bill. You'll make a great mother."

He hadn't answered the crucial question she lacked the courage to ask. He must know what she wanted. What she needed. She tried a different approach. "Tell me why I should marry you."

Nicholas gave her a puzzled frown. "I'd think that was obvious. You've harped on it yourself. You're twenty-seven years old. I'm offering you a husband and a family."

"You think I should marry you because I'm desperate? Did it ever occur to you, Nicholas Bonelli, that what you're offering may not be enough for me?"

"I know you aren't talking about money." Bewilderment filled his eyes. "What more do you want?"

"Love. I want love."

Nicholas turned to stone.

Shadows crept down the street as the sun descended

toward the peaks of the Front Range. The car, parked in the shade of a large spruce tree, had lost its warmth, and the metal pressed coldly against Rachel's back. The street stood quiet, the neighbors in their houses, eating dinner or watching television. Even the dogs and cats had disappeared. The setting sun disappeared over the hills with one last burst of rays. A hummingbird whistled past, piercing the taut silence.

"I want to sleep with you, but it's more than that," Nicholas said. "You're the first woman I've known whom I've considered marrying and raising a family with." He curved his hand along the side of her face. "I wish I'd met you years ago, Teach. I wish I could say I loved you." He caressed her cheek with his thumb. "I wish I could love you as you deserve to be loved. But I can't. It's too late for me to fall in love."

"It's never too late to fall in love."

"It is when you're a Bonelli."

She shook off his hand. It didn't matter that he spoke total nonsense. Not when he believed it. One day he'd fall in love. He just wouldn't fall in love with her.

He waited for her answer.

She'd set out to clear her father. Instead she'd learned a hard and ugly truth. Happiness could still be hers. All she had to do was say yes to Nicholas. But at what cost to him? Her answer came haltingly past a throat raw from crying. "No. I can't marry you." Marrying her would destroy any chance Nicholas ever had of finding a woman to love. Rachel couldn't do that to him. She loved him too much.

The car moving slowly down the street toward them came to a stop. Tony leaned out the open car window. "You must be Bonelli. Mom said you needed a ride home. She doesn't want Rachel driving in the state she's in. Hop in." When Nicholas didn't move, Tony added, "Don't worry. Mom told me what happened so I won't sock you for making Rachel cry.'' He frowned at his sister. ''You look a mess. You okay?''

''Why didn't you tell me, Tony?''

''C'mon, Rache, as far as I'm concerned, it's yesterday's news. How was I supposed to know it mattered to you?''

''You're the son of a criminal.''

Tony shrugged. ''So? Larceny isn't something you inherit like red hair. Besides—'' he grinned boyishly ''—sometimes a little wickedness on the family tree works better on women than etchings, if you know what I mean.''

Nicholas laughed and went around the front of Tony's car and climbed in the passenger side. Her brother drove away.

And just like that Nicholas was riding out of Rachel's life. Leaving her. Because he couldn't love her.

Tony made a U-turn at the bottom of the street and pulled up again beside Rachel. Nicholas thrust his good hand out the open car window, a white square held in his fingers. ''My phone numbers. Work and home. If you change your mind...''

Rachel put her hands behind her back, rejecting the card. Rejecting temptation. She wouldn't change her mind. Swallowing hard, determined not to break down again in front of him, she hid her secret behind a wall of pride. ''I won't change my mind. Some day you'll be grateful I said no. You'll meet a woman who has the qualities you want and you'll fall in love.''

''I won't fall in love,'' he said harshly. ''And I found the woman who has what I want. I meant what I said to your mother about you. You're tough and brave.'' His voice softened. ''I can see my children nursing at your breast, playing at your feet. I can see you teaching them to read and write and bake cookies and laugh. I can see you teaching them about caring and loyalty and courage.

I'm sorry you can't see those same things." He gestured to Tony and they drove away. This time they didn't return.

Rachel wrapped her arms around herself and rocked back and forth in the street. She wanted to chase after him screaming she could see them. This intense pain slashing her to pieces must be how her mother felt after Rachel's father had abandoned them. Wondering how she could continue without him. Seeing ahead the bleakness of her days. Life without Nicholas. She looked down. A single tear blotted the white card at Rachel's feet.

"The way you two were bickering when I walked into the kitchen," her mother said behind her, "I wondered if there was something between you."

"Now you know." There was nothing. Rachel wiped her nose with Nicholas's balled-up handkerchief. His handkerchief and the memory of a few kisses were all she had left of Nicholas.

"Does his family mind?" Mrs. Stuart put her arm around Rachel's shoulders and guided her back toward the house.

"About what?" Rachel asked, not really caring. She wanted to go to her own apartment to curl up and die, but she didn't have the strength to throw off her mother's arm.

"That he's in love with you. His father seemed nice the one time I met him, so I imagine it'll be okay. Has he asked you to marry him yet?"

Rachel stood stock-still and stared blindly at her mother. "I told him no."

Her mother gave her a perplexed frown. "I could have sworn you loved him."

Her mother's words reactivated the river of tears. "I think I fell in love with him the minute I saw him. He was encased in plaster, oh, it's fiberglass these days, but still, I thought he was the sexiest man I'd ever seen. There's something about a wounded hero.'' She smiled through her tears. "Not that he wasn't as grumpy as a two-year-old who needed a nap. He saved my life when I fell off the dock and almost drowned in the lake. You should see him with children and dogs. He's kind and firm and gentle and caring. He has such beautiful brown eyes,'' she added dreamily. "Did you see his eyes?''

Without waiting for her mother to answer, she continued, "He's strong and assertive and masculine. I love his laugh, and his smile turns me to melted blubber. He's nice-looking, don't you think? I never knew I'd like curly dark hair.''

"I don't understand why you turned him down.''

The warmth faded from Rachel's memories. "He doesn't love me. He said so.''

Mrs. Stuart laughed softly. "And you believe him? After what he hollered out the car window?''

"It doesn't matter what I believe,'' Rachel said hollowly. "He believes it.''

Mrs. Stuart drew herself up to her full height. "Rachel Sarah Stuart. I thought I taught you better than this. Standing out here where all the neighbors can see you and crying like a weak sissy. If you love him, quit feeling sorry for yourself and do something about it.''

A week later Rachel stood in the foyer of Addison and Bonelli scowling down at the dog grinning up at her. "I cannot believe I agreed to take you while the McDonnells flew back east for a family funeral. If you hadn't destroyed Mother's favorite rosebush I could have left you in her backyard. And if you hadn't eaten all the cookies Tony's girlfriend baked him yesterday, I could have convinced Tony to take you, at least for the afternoon. I swear, Scotty, if you ruin this for me, I'll... I don't know what I'll do, but you won't like it.''

Rachel settled her hat squarely on her head, patted the mass of curls falling to her shoulders, unbuttoned the three top buttons of her gold lamé, skintight dress, and wrapped the leash tighter around her palm. "Please, Scotty, just this once, do as I ask." She opened the door into Nicholas's outer office.

A middle-aged woman looked up, her eyes widening at the exotic sight in the doorway. "Yes?"

"I got an appointment with Nicky," Rachel said, dragging Scotty, who'd discovered a water cooler, into the room. She had an awful feeling Scotty thought the water cooler served the same purpose as a fire hydrant.

"I'm sorry." The woman didn't sound sorry. "There must be some mistake. Mr. Bonelli has a meeting scheduled."

"Yeah, with Charlie." Pushing Scotty to the floor, Rachel perched a golden hip on the woman's desk and confided, "Charlie's swell. He set this up for me 'cuz Nicky's been acting like a dope." She winked at the transfixed woman. "You know how it is." Rachel pulled a compact out of her huge tote bag.

"I don't know how it is," the woman said coolly.

Rachel stopped powdering her nose. "You mean you got a guy who isn't full of screwy notions? Hang on to him, sister." She snapped her compact shut. "You gonna announce me or do I just bust in on Nicky?"

"Really, Ms. Whoever-you-are, I think you've made a mistake."

Rachel yanked Scotty away from his investigation of the woman's leg. "Nicky calls me Dollface. Me and him is—" she winked again "—you know."

The woman stared at her fascinated. "You and Nick?" She pushed Scotty away from her.

"Yeah. I know. Hard to figure. He can be a louse, but he's a handsome louse."

The woman shook her head as if to clear it. "Maybe I better call security."

"Better not. Scotty hates coppers." She couldn't imagine Scotty hating anyone. Unsnapping the young dog's leash, Rachel reached into her bag and took out his huge, hard rubber toy which she slung across the room. The toy thudded off the closed door leading into Nicholas's private office. Yelping hysterically in delight, Scotty raced after the ball. His enormous feet hadn't mastered the art of braking and he careened into the door.

By the time Nicholas yanked open the door, Scotty was back on his leash and Rachel was again perched on the desk. She peered up at Nicholas from under her wide-brimmed hat. "Hiya, gumshoe. Your guardian angel here is threatening to call the coppers on me." She added in a throaty voice, "Why don't you square things with her and then you can frisk me yourself."

Scotty bolted across the room toward Nicholas. Unfortunately his leash was wrapped around Rachel's hand. Before Rachel could release the puppy, she found herself flung headlong against Nicholas's hard body. He caught her with his good arm.

"Get down."

She wrapped her free arm around his neck. "I hope you're talking to Scotty."

Nicholas's mouth twitched. "If you're here to trace this fellow's pedigree—yes, Scotty, hello, there's a good boy, be quiet—even with our resources, I doubt it can be done."

"I know his pedigree. He's part police dog, part bloodhound and part Cupid."

Nicholas's gaze sharpened. "Interesting. Perhaps we should discuss it in private." Taking her hand from his neck, he looked over her hat. "I don't want to be disturbed. By anyone. Perhaps you'd keep the dog...ah, perhaps not." His gaze returned to Rachel. "I assume you're here to see me?"

"You are a clever gumshoe, aren't you?"

"Not clever enough to figure you out." He ushered Rachel and Scotty into the room and shut the door. "Lay down."

Again Rachel assumed he referred to the dog. Opening her tote bag, she pulled out a plastic sack and dumped a huge soup bone in one corner of the office. This time she remembered to release Scotty first.

She dusted off her hands. "Now. About this little investigation I've been working on for you, Boss."

Nicholas leaned back in his office chair. He bent his uninjured arm behind his head. "I like the boss bit."

Rachel batted her eyes at him. "I said that in case your office is bugged, Nicky, darling."

"The only thing bugged in here is me, wondering what's going on."

Moving around his desk, Rachel shunted aside papers and a fishbowl. She slanted him a teasing look. "I'm not sure Ian would approve of a hotshot detective owning a goldfish."

"He was a gift from JoJo and Andy."

"Swell." She sat on the desk's edge near his chair. Judging by the look in his eyes, Nicholas noticed the way her skirt rode up exposing nylon-clad thighs. She casually crossed her legs and tossed the large tote on his desk. "It's all here, Nicky. I found her."

"Her?"

"Nicky, darling, think! The Bonelli legend—or curse, depending on one's point of view."

His eyes narrowed. "What the hell's going on, Rachel?"

"Don't be cross, Nicky." She threw out her lower lip in an exaggerated pout. "You said you had to fall in love at an early age. Well, it turns out you did."

"And I don't remember that, because?"

Rachel gave him a wide-eyed look of innocence. "Accidents. Can you believe it?"

"No."

"Nicky, darling, don't sulk. You're always telling me hotshot detectives don't go looking for facts to prove a pet theory. That they keep an open mind until they see what the facts tell them." She gave him a ingenuous smile. "So, to find out why you were such a blot on the old Bonelli escutcheon, I started at the very beginning to see what would turn up. And look."

She pulled a photograph from the bag. One baby blew a bubble of saliva at the camera from a hospital crib. The baby in an adjoining crib looked solemnly over at the first. "Aren't they precious?" Rachel crooned. "It was love at first sight."

Nicholas picked up the photograph and gave it a casual glance. He started to set it down, then gave it closer scrutiny. "I've seen a picture like this before, except there was only one baby in it. Me. I've never seen this photo with the other kid. I wouldn't have forgotten that curly hair. Who is he?"

"She. Your first love. Apparently you couldn't keep your eyes off her. If the picture was in color, you'd see why."

"Would I?"

Rachel coyly patted her hair. "Red curls."

"I see. You appear to have more pictures."

"Mr. Hotshot Detective," she teased.

He studied the picture she handed him. "My first day of school. In living color. The little redhead I'm grinning at?"

"Her first day, too. You were crazy about her."

"I don't remember her."

"Do you remember falling off the monkey bars?" At

his nod, Rachel said, "Amnesia." She handed him another picture.

"Halloween. I must have been about eight. I was a pirate. Cute redhaired little fairy princess."

"Look at the way you're holding her hand. Young love is so touching."

"I don't remember her."

"You remember Dyan learning how to play softball and throwing the bat and hitting you in the head?"

"Causing amnesia again?"

"Exactly." She dug in the tote for another photo.

"Waiting for the school bus on my first day of high school. I suppose I was crazy about that red-haired girl standing there."

"The first girl you kissed," Rachel said fondly. "You didn't even mind the braces and all the freckles." At his look of inquiry, she added, "Football injury."

"Ah, the concussion."

She nodded and handed him another picture. "High school prom. Gosh, you were handsome in your rented tuxedo."

He squinted at the picture. "I see the redhead got her braces off."

"She still had freckles."

"And?"

"Remember your skiing accident? You and Dyan were racing down the slope and she fell in front of you and you hit a tree to avoid hitting her?"

"I broke my leg, but I don't remember having a concussion or losing my memory."

Rachel shook her head sadly. "Post-trauma amnesia."

"Of course." He held out his hand for another picture. "College graduation." He stared critically at the photograph. "You haven't changed much. That pink dress was a bad color for you. You look better in this gold thing."

"How sweet, Nicky. I didn't think you'd noticed."

His gaze traveled slowly over multistrapped ridiculously high sandals, up shimmering legs and thighs, past form-fitting lamé and stopped at the cleavage exposed by the indecently low neckline. "I noticed. Interesting. You blush all over, don't you? Well?"

"I don't, I mean, maybe I do, but it's rude of you to—"

"I meant, what's the reason I don't remember you at graduation?"

"The sailing incident. One of those masts or something hit you in the head. Really, Nicholas," she said severely, "you've been leading a life entirely too fraught with peril."

He gave her a dry look. "I have a feeling I've never been in as much peril as I'm in right now. That the end of the pictures?"

Rachel suddenly found the blank wall behind Nicholas's head of enormous interest. "I guess that's up to you." She nervously crossed and uncrossed her legs. "You thought you couldn't fall in love because you didn't fall in love when you were younger. I mean, that is the Bonelli legacy. The thing is—" she swung her legs faster "—you were wrong. You fell in love when you were a few days' old and remained remarkably constant to your true love. Even if you don't remember her."

The sound of Scotty gnawing on his bone sounded incredibly loud in the ominously quiet office.

"And you?"

Gathering every ounce of courage she possessed, Rachel looked straight at Nicholas and said in a soft, firm voice, "From the moment I saw him, I've been totally, completely, unalterably constant to my true love."

Nicholas looked steadily back at her. "You're eight

years younger than me. How could we possibly have been in the hospital nursery at the same time or started school on the same day?''

Rachel almost shriveled up and died then, thinking she'd gambled and lost. Then she saw the look in Nicholas's eyes. Her lips slowly curved in a wide, provocative smile. "Through the miracle of love," she purred.

Nicholas raised an eyebrow. "Don't you mean the miracle of computer-altered photographs?"

Rachel's heart sunk. She'd misinterpreted the light in his eyes. "Can't fool the hotshot detective, can I?" Her smile wobbled only a little. "Well, I've had my fun, so I guess we can go. At least you have to admit Scotty's been well behaved today."

"You call it well behaved when he knocks over a vaseful of flowers so he can drink the water? You call it well behaved when he goes to the bathroom on my office rug? You call it well behaved when he dumps over the wastebasket, chews on the leg of my sofa and destroys two throw pillows?"

Rachel turned and looked with horror on the devastation Scotty had wrought behind her back. Feathers and shredded papers and dying flowers littered the expensive carpet. "Oh, no! How did he do that without me noticing?" In the corner Scotty slept like a canine angel with his head on the bone between his front paws. "I'm sorry. I'll clean it up right now."

"Haven't you forgotten something?" Nicholas stood up.

"I don't think so." Rachel edged backward as Nicholas loomed over her.

He planted a fist on the desk. "You invited me to frisk you, remember?" he asked in a mild voice. "Or do you have bouts of amnesia, too?" He bent toward her.

Rachel panicked, leaned away from him, lost her balance and pitched backward, hitting the edge of the goldfish bowl as she fell. It toppled over, dumping the contents down the front of her dress. "Get him off me!"

Nicholas laughed so hard he had trouble retrieving the goldfish flopping between Rachel's breasts. Even drenched with cool water, Rachel felt Nicholas's every knuckle brush against her supersensitive skin.

He plopped the fish back into the bowl, and took it over to the door where he handed it through a opened crack with a few words. He turned to see Rachel standing beside the desk and shook his head. "My sister has a lot to answer for."

She couldn't blame Nicholas for being disgusted. He must be giving thanks she'd turned down his marriage proposal. She couldn't blame him for that, either. She'd wanted to prove to Nicholas once and for all the silliness of his family's credo that the only true love was young love. Her grand idea had turned into a total debacle. His office looked like a Chinook wind had roared through. "I'm sorry." She wiped ineffectively at the water dripping down her onto the carpet.

He stalked over and roughly brushed aside her hands. "Get out of that dress. You're soaked."

"I'm not going to..." She stopped at the militant look in his eyes. "I don't have anything to put on."

Nicholas pointed to a gym bag sitting on the floor by Scotty. "There's a towel and a sweatshirt in there. And don't wake up the damned dog." He faced away from her. "You've got one minute."

"I can't change in a minute."

"I'll be happy to help you by removing the dress," he said in a silky voice.

Pointedly turning her back to him, Rachel removed it herself. Along with her sodden bra. Fortunately the water had confined itself to her upper half. Leaving her clothing heaped on the floor, she scrambled into a dark green sweatshirt after a cursory wipe with the towel. Not knowing where to put her hat, she plopped it back on her head. The sweatshirt reached to the top of her thighs. She tried to yank it down further.

"I love the shoes, but the hat has got to go."

She whirled. Nicholas was walking toward her with a look which could only be described as predatory in his eyes. "Don't you like it?" she asked, for lack of anything better to say.

Nicholas didn't bother to look down as he strode through the mess on the floor. "It's in my way." Lifting the hat from her head, he flung it to one side.

The hat sailed across the room and landed on Scotty. The dog wakened instantly, leaping to his feet and wagging his tail enthusiastically. With a single bound, he was across the floor and up on his hind legs licking Rachel's face. It was the last straw. Rachel pushed Scotty to the floor, bundled up her clothing and towed the dog toward the office door. "I'll return your things to Dyan," she said in a choked voice. "Send me the bill for cleaning your office."

"Forget it. You're not blowing this joint until me and you square things up between us." Laughter filled Nicholas's voice. Laughter and something else. He hauled Scotty to the door and opened it. Charlie's voice rumbled from the other side.

Nicholas shut the office door. "Charlie's calling Dyan. Scotty can go play with JoJo and Andy. She deserves him."

Rachel looked away from eyes gleaming with laughter. "Because it was her idea to stick you up in Grand Lake."

"That's right." He wrapped an arm around her hips, pulling her to him. "Last week I asked you to marry me."

Did he think she could possibly have forgotten? She studied the light tan stripes in his white shirt. "I remember."

"You turned me down."

"Yes." Someone had sewed one of his buttons back on crooked. Ask me again, she begged silently. She knew how to sew on buttons.

"I'm glad you did."

His words didn't hurt. They couldn't hurt. Her entire body had gone numb. She forced air into her lungs, praying for strength. She needed it. Badly. She wasn't a sissy. She wasn't. Words. She needed words. Words to convince him she didn't care. "I told you one day you'd be grateful." She didn't expect it so soon. Her mother was wrong. He didn't love her.

Nicholas trailed his hand over the curve of her hip. "Aren't you going to ask me why I'm glad?"

Mutely she shook her head. The sweatshirt had ridden up and only the thinnest of panty hose separated her skin from his hand.

Silent laughter shook him. "For one thing, I would have missed this."

"This?" She wanted to dissolve into the palm of his hand.

"The Dollface outfit." He chuckled. "The goldfish."

His laughter dented her control. She had to get out of here before she burst into tears. If only his hand didn't feel so right on her hip. Coming had been a mistake. "I'm sorry." Sorry for the mess. Sorry he couldn't love her.

"Don't be. It was the best thing that ever happened to me. If you'd said yes, I might never have fallen in love."

He'd found someone else. She hadn't known words could wound so fiercely. She should have said yes. He'd be hers. Except he wouldn't. Not when he didn't love her. She forced speech past an aching throat. "Love is like that. It happens quick." She ought to know.

"Not so quick. I didn't even notice. It took a major disaster before I realized what had happened."

"Your injuries." She wondered which one of his women friends he meant.

"Worse than that." He tipped up her head. "A red-headed woman refused to marry me." Uncertainty flickered in the back of his eyes. "Tell me I'm not too late to change her mind."

Her breath caught. Nicholas Bonelli uncertain about anything? He wasn't the only one. "I'm not sure what you mean."

"All week I struggled with my feelings. Told myself I only felt physical attraction. That I was annoyed because you rejected me. Tried to convince myself I wanted you in my bed, not in my heart." His hand tightened around her hip. "I was lying to myself. That's why I'm glad you refused to marry me."

"But I thought... You just asked me again," Rachel said, thoroughly bewildered. "Didn't you?"

"For different reasons. For the right reasons. If you'd said yes before I might never have admitted the truth."

"The truth," she repeated stupidly.

"I don't want to marry you because you fit the bill." He framed her face with his hand. "I want to marry you because I'm crazy in love with you."

"What about the family tradition of young love?"

"What about it? Haven't you just proved we met in our cradles?"

She concentrated on his healing scar. "Are you sure you aren't thinking of the other part to the tradition? Marrying in the teeth of opposition? What about my father? And yours?"

"I don't give a damn about your father. As for mine, he'll never be able to resist redheaded grandkids." He lightly kissed her trembling mouth. "Say yes, Rachel. Love me. Call me 'Nicky, darling' for the rest of our lives."

So much joy and happiness filled her heart, if she fell in the lake right now, she'd float. Pinning a scowl on her face, she looked Nicholas right in the eye. "Listen, gumshoe, ya been a louse, but I kinda got a yen for ya, see, so if this proposal ain't no song and dance and you're on the level—Nicky, darling, be careful! Your shoulder!"

Take 4 bestselling love stories FREE

Plus get a FREE surprise gift!

FIVE STARS
MEAN SUCCESS

**If you see the "5 Star Club" flash on a book,
it means we're introducing you to one of our
most STELLAR authors!**

Every one of our Harlequin and Silhouette
authors who has sold over 5 MILLION BOOKS
has been selected for our "5 Star Club."

We've created the club so you won't miss
any of our bestsellers. So, each month
we'll be highlighting every original book within
Harlequin and Silhouette written by our
bestselling authors.

NOW THERE'S NO WAY ON EARTH OUR
STARS WON'T BE SEEN!

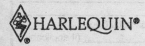 

P5STAR

Our **5 Star Club** authors are successful authors who have sold **over 5 million books**. In honor of their success, we're offering you a <u>FREE</u> gift and a chance to look like a million bucks!

You can choose:

the necklace...

the bracelet...

or the earrings...

Or indulge, and receive all three!

To receive one item, send in 1 (one)* proof of purchase, plus $1.65 U.S./$2.25 CAN. for postage and handling, to:

In the U.S.
Harlequin 5 Star Club
3010 Walden Ave.
P.O. Box 9047
Buffalo, NY
14269-9047

In Canada
Harlequin 5 Star Club
P.O. Box 636
Fort Erie, Ontario
L2A 5X3

* To receive more than one piece of jewelry, send in another proof of purchase and an additional 25¢ for each extra item.

5 STAR CLUB—
PROOF OF PURCHASE

Inventory:	Item:	
721-1	Necklace	☐
722-9	Bracelet	☐
723-7	Earrings	☐

Name: _____
Address: _____
City: _____
State/Prov.: _____ Zip/Postal Code: _____
Account number:_____ (if applicable)

093 KGI CCY6   ◆HARLEQUIN®

093 KGI CCY6